D0536586

The Last Photograph

The Last Photograph

SIMON ASTAIRE

SPELLBINDING
M E D I A

LONDON

Published by Spellbinding Media 2013

First published in Great Britain in 2013 by
Spellbinding Media
17 Empress Place
London SW6 1TT
www.spellbindingmedia.co.uk

Spellbinding Media Ltd Reg. No. 08482364
A CIP catalogue record for this book is available from the British Library

ISBN 9781909964006

Typeset in Adobe Garamond by ForDesign, London
Printed and bound by TJ International Ltd, Padstow, Cornwall

for Edgar and Lesley

Acknowledgements

Margaret Weisz for inspiring part of this story.
Michael Mainwaring for his quotes
and notes on grief. Bless you

When you are sorrowful, look again in your heart,
and you shall see that in truth you are weeping
for that which has been your delight.

Kahlil Gibran (1883-1931): *The Prophet*

I

I'd assumed the end was the end. Not an end that led to a beginning, nor an affirmation of the fact that none of us truly arrive.

∴

The alarm rang at seven o'clock. That is to say, it would have rung had I not woken up some eight minutes earlier and pressed the little tit on the top of the clock, thereby averting the sound of the bell that, because of my age, would've been as startling as a wartime siren. During those eight minutes, however, my greatest joy was peace of mind and nothing was more valuable. I drifted off into a deep doze, in which I dreamed I hadn't pressed the alarm at all. Only when I thought I heard a faint *click* like that of a safety catch being released or the trigger of an unloaded gun being pulled, did I remember that I'd pressed the alarm clock button – and only when I opened my eyes did I remember another, rather significant, fact: which was, that I did not possess an alarm clock at all.

The supposed event had been the horseplay of my mind. There was no safety catch, no trigger. My mind had begun to act without boundaries; to control it, I was getting into the habit of ordering it to do things.

Like, *Wake up now!* and *Time to brush your teeth*.

As long as I can remember, I've been a deep sleeper. No sleeping pills for me. If sleepers are divided between those who open their eyes at a letter being slid under a door and those who can sleep through a declaration of war; between those who can only rest comfortably in their own bed, and those who can put their heads back and fall asleep anywhere – well, I belong to the latter group.

I drank one cup of coffee, washed, shaved and dressed almost mechanically. I thought about having breakfast but decided to wait until after I'd visited the bank, by which time an early morning appetite would have been born of a short walk and the fresh air. I picked up yesterday's paper from the kitchen table, held it in one hand and carried my new khaki canvas bag, with its Union Jack patch, in the other. I locked the front door, put the keys in the bag, checked my watch, exclaimed, 'My God, is that the time?' and set about the day.

The weather was sultry. A vagrant, nervously fanning himself with a newspaper, created the only hint of breeze. He was sitting, or rather he was lying propped up against the main entrance of the building. His feet were splayed out at right angles. Colonel Weldon, the chairman of our building's residents' committee, was taking aim at the poor soul. He was about to kick him into the gutter with his big right foot, when he was interrupted mid-air by my breezy voice.

'Good morning, Colonel!'

'Ah! Good morning, Hammond. I think it's going to be another bloody hot day.'

'Already is, Colonel,' I replied.

'It's like the damn tropics! Did you know the body rots so much quicker out there? It reminds me of this journalist who went missing after a quick bevvy in the local bar … You know, when they found him he was already embalmed, with local cotton wool up his arse!'

Colonel Weldon was unshaven. He didn't have a beard, so much as he had elongated facial hair known in some circles as grippers. When I'd first arrived at the building, he'd marched over to shake my hand. His handshake was firm enough to make it clear he was in command, but brief enough to show he was not the least bit intimidated by me or anyone else he encountered.

He asked a few non-sequitur questions and then paused. The silence was meant to be menacing, so I shuffled uneasily but then I grew irritated. Last year he had asked whether I would be interested in joining the residents' committee. I'd thought about it for around a second and then politely refused.

Since then I've had little to do with him.

'Well, Colonel,' I interrupted. 'I really should be going, I've an appointment at the bank.'

It was a white lie. All I had to do was withdraw some funds from the ATM machine. The money was owed to my inefficient plumber, Colin, who called late the previous evening to say he'd pop by the shop just after eleven o'clock to pick up the cash for my new boiler, which was temperamental (aren't they all?).

'You'd better follow me,' I whispered to the vagrant, sparing him a hefty bruise in the groin.

He peered at me inquisitively, then stood up with probably the same ease as he'd sat down. He licked his lips and, judging by the general state of his health (especially the glazed eyes and deep notches in his pockmarked skin), was in need of a good meal.

'Come on. Keep up!' I urged.

His face creased and his nose twitched as if he could smell bread being baked somewhere. He then tagged along, swaying from side to side. When we were out of view of the Colonel, I turned.

'Here, treat yourself to some breakfast and have a shave.'

I handed over twenty pounds.

He seemed flattered and puzzled. 'You must be rich,' he laughed.

'I'm not.'

'Well, you act as if you are,' he said, grinning to reveal a mouthful of chaotic teeth. 'I've always known that's one of life's secrets: to act rich, even if you're not.'

He hawked loudly and spat on the ground. His spit was not white, I can tell you that. As I walked away, I noticed him checking the twenty-pound note in the morning sunlight.

∴

At the bank, several lines had formed in front of the cash machines. There were usually three in operation but that day it was reduced to one. I joined what I thought was the principal line and got immediately accused of cutting in.

'Get to the back!' shouted a moaner who seemed to be the one most guilty of the offence himself. The heat wasn't helping matters. A bank official came out to try to calm things down, but his appearance and tone made everybody shove more rigorously.

In the struggle, I was barged over.

Now, there is one advantage in being seen as a little older: when you fall to the ground, the instinct of others is to help you. I was somewhat dazed, to such an extent that a stray cat passing by seemed to bark *ruff!* at me.

'Are you all right?' asked the bank official, looking worried.

'Fine. I'm just fine,' I said, perhaps too hastily. The crowd sighed with relief and quickly reformed the line. I was helped to my feet by a man with silver hair, a silver face but tanned all over. I half expected him to be wearing silver pants with a silver buckle and silver boots, but I was to be disappointed.

'An old boy like you should be more careful,' he said, walking the tightrope between courtesy and familiarity.

'Hey, enough of the old boy! I'm only sixty-eight.'

'Sixty-eight? What the heck have you been doing to yourself?'

He let out a chuckle, offering me his arm like a carer does an elderly relative. In his left hand, he held my canvas bag.

'They call this a man-bag these days,' he said.

'Do they?'

When I'd regained my balance, he placed the bag onto my forearm. I rubbed the dirt off my hands. As I did so, I thought of how small and weak they seemed.

Mr Khan, the bank manager, now took over.

'You'd better follow me,' he said.

Compared to the hubbub outside, the bank was quiet. Like a morgue. I was sliding across the polished floor as Mr Khan guided me to a sea-green leather chair in the far corner, beneath a portrait of the Duke of Wellington. The scene was not particularly attractive.

I felt as if I was bouncing off one wall, spread-eagling my way to another, and then back again. I laughed at the ridiculousness of it all. Was it the laughter of fear? Finally, and I believe only by chance, I found myself collapsing into the chair.

'Ah that's better,' I said.

'Look at the state of you,' Mr Khan said.

'What did you say?'

'I said, what can I do for you?'

'I need five hundred pounds in cash.'

Mr Khan nodded, took a deep breath and said, 'In fifties okay, Mr Hammond?'

'Yes, fifties would be fine.'

Mr Khan had been my bank manager for five years. He was a rather insipid man who, when I once asked him why people thought bank managers were as unpopular as estate agents, gave the dullest of answers. He was the type who would not move from his fence, preferring to sit with his legs dangling over whichever side he thought the more appropriate or more interesting at the time. On the rare occasions he decided to step down off that fence, he did something stupid and therefore soon climbed back to his already warmed position.

He should've been more careful. If you sit too hard on the fence of life, you're liable to split yourself down the middle.

'Five hundred pounds, Mr Hammond.'

I thanked him and put the brown envelope deep into my bag.

'Anything else, Mr Hammond?'

'Not for now, but I may come in next week.'

'Unfortunately I won't be here then, sir. It's my annual holiday.'

'Anywhere nice?' I asked.

'Yes,' he replied matter-of-factly, as if it was nobody's business, especially mine. 'I'm going to a currency conference in Istanbul.'

How odd, I thought. *Isn't that what they call a busman's holiday?*

'Have a marvellous time,' I said.

As I walked out, I saw the line of people waiting for the ATM hadn't diminished.

'I'd try inside if I were you," I told them. "Ask for a Mr Khan.'

The people looked at each other and then rushed forward, barging past me, swinging open the doors and nearly crushing my hand.

'Mind out!' I shouted. But no one took a blind bit of notice.

∴

An organic restaurant had recently opened in the neighbourhood. Probably because I ran the bookshop next door, the owner Hannah had made a courteous opening day visit and had invited me in for a free smoothie.

'It's the speciality of the house,' she said. 'I'd go for the one called berry nice. It's my favourite by far.'

I liked Hannah, who was what I'd call nicely upholstered and searingly attractive to a man of my age. She was always welcoming and, when I took out my money, she would say with her omnipresent smile, 'there's no need for you to pay.' In return I would drop off a nice, long novel to get into.

One evening I bumped into her when I was in my local pub.

'Hello. I'm not bothering you, am I?' she asked.

'Why would you be bothering me?'

Funny, being older doesn't stop that immediate male reaction of wanting to charm someone, thinking you might have a chance of making an impression; for a moment, I flattered myself that she was thrilled to spend time with me.

'Are you alone?' I asked.

'I'm meeting someone but I'm a little early,' Hannah replied.

'Come and sit down while you wait.'

She thanked me and I went up to the bar to order her a gin and tonic. When I returned, there was a long pause until I broke the silence.

'Who are you meeting?'

Another pause.

'Sorry,' I said. 'That was very forward of me.'

It was none of my business. I usually hate that over-familiar banter from others.

'I'm meeting my sister,' she said, smiling for no other reason than it was natural for her.

Wow, you are lovely, I thought.

'Are you the older one?' I asked.

'Yes, by quite a bit. I'm a sort of mother to her.'

I had no real idea what she meant, but I nodded as if I did. I examined her with great care, almost pecking at her. She probably thought I was either very interested, myopic, or both.

'When we lost both our parents at a young age, I brought her up.'

'That must have been difficult.'

Hannah forced a smile in a way that showed the memory still lingered and hurt.

I recognised that look.

'It was the night before my seventeenth birthday,' she went on. 'There we were, discussing where we were going to lunch the following day and a few hours later, I was identifying their bodies.'

She spoke calmly, in a matter-of-fact manner.

'They were driving home from a dinner party," she continued, 'when my father misjudged a corner. It was one of those country roads with no lights, dark, a wood on either side …'

'Hannah!'

Her name hung over the table. It was her sister. As she walked towards us, Hannah whispered to me.

'Sorry. I don't usually go there.'

'You have nothing to be sorry about,' I said, leaning forward and quickly squeezing her hand, pulling my own back sharply before her sister could see.

Her sister didn't look younger. They looked more like twins. I immediately made an excuse and said I must be going, but Hannah insisted she bought me a drink.

'Thank you,' I replied.

Hannah's sister was distracted. She kept shifting a phone, her purse and a pen around the table. She clearly wanted to be alone with Hannah.

I hurried my drink along. I learned they'd both gone to a private school in Kent and hated it.

'Where in Kent?' I asked.

'Broadstairs,' the sister said.

'I know it well,' I replied.

'You do?' She sounded very surprised.

'Yes, my son went to a school nearby.'

But instead of asking which one, the sister said, 'Terrible place Broadstairs. Full of gloom.'

'Really? I think it's rather beautiful.'

'Bad memories,' she said, and then Hannah interrupted the conversation like a mother does when you're talking too much.

I used the moment to get up and say my goodbyes.

'We should do this again sometime,' Hannah said.

'I would love that,' I replied and then turned to her sister. 'You should be proud of Hannah. Her restaurant has changed the whole feeling of the street, for the better.'

'I am very proud of her,' she replied without hesitation.

∴

I'd made a habit of stopping off at Hannah's restaurant at the start of each new day. It had become something of a treat. I always chose the corner table that stared out of the window onto the street. I tried to be there without being there; like someone walking across snow without leaving any footprints.

'How are you today, Tom?' asked Hannah.

'I'm very well. It's good to see you're so busy,' I answered, and was about to comment on how lovely she looked, when I was interrupted by tut-tutting coming from a woman on the next table.

She was staring at two students who were sharing a cigarette.

'I don't know why they still smoke," she said. 'And at this time of the morning! They must know they are killing themselves?'

The woman's face was full of suspicion, like someone who'd been told she'd won something but reckoned a load of other people had been told exactly the same thing.

'Maybe they smoke to relieve themselves from the drudgery of life and to soothe the ache of change,' I said.

The woman hesitated, looking at me for several quizzical seconds.

'Rubbish!' she spat. 'What do you know about the young?'

'Very little I suppose,' I answered her.

She huffed at this, then burst into a speech like someone on Speaker's Corner.

'Freedom to kill yourself is,' she began, 'some would claim, an integral ingredient of true democracy. But let's at least be obliged to commit the act in specially designated areas, if only so as not to spread the smoke, sickness and self-disgust …'

The woman had seen the opportunity to remark on all the comings and goings of the area, and add a lame joke about the deluge of rubbish that had grown due to a recent strike. In the past I might have listened and felt honour-bound to join in, or to at least smile.

But not these days, I thought.

Just as my breakfast was arriving I got up, left some cash on the table and walked next door to open the bookshop, my stomach still empty.

∴

I was without the help of Charles, my assistant, who had left the day before for his annual summer break. Charles, who I regularly advised to relax and not try to solve the major issues of the world.

'Concentrate and specialise on what you reckon you can do best,' I would say to him.

Charles had been working for me for about six years. I had grown to like him enormously. In fact, I depended on him. Our relationship had gradually changed, though. He now ordered the stock, advised when the shop window should be updated, and when to organise book signings by authors. I wasn't sure as to when, exactly, our roles had switched. I'd been thinking how or when this happens; how difficult it is to define these pinpoints of time.

Have you ever tried going to sleep by attempting to remember the last second you were awake? Or maybe it's more like, if one person chases another person in a circle, and that other person is running an iota faster, there comes a time when the chaser is the chased. Yes that's more like it, that's how it is: when the pursuer is being pursued.

Maybe that defines most of my relationships in these last years.

My instinct to take full control of my life was slowly diminishing, and it seemed a little early for that. When I spoke to my pharmacist about it, he advised me to eat royal jelly because, he said, it helps the power of concentration.

'That's your problem. You're not concentrating like you used to.'

He was right. My concentration had begun to wane. I was making a conscious effort to recognise the fact and not succumb to its threat. I was always a good listener but recently words had started to sound mixed up. My mind had sped so out of control that I took someone's last word to be his or her first and believed it to sound like an order, which I was repeatedly on the verge of obeying.

On the bright side, I was aware that confusion was shadowing me, and I was determined to stem the tide.

'You're going on a cruise, eh, Charles? What, on one of those amusement-saturated ships?' I asked, not quite believing him when he told me where he was going to spend his weeks off.

'Yes, isn't that exciting?'

'Ah no! They've had their day, haven't they?'

'I believe not. I'm going with a pile of books and will enjoy reading them as we pass through Norwegian fjords. I don't need anything else. As someone once said, a book is still the greatest one-to-one encounter between two human beings.'

'Who said that?'

'I think I just did.'

'That's a fine quote. We should send it in to *The Oxford Dictionary of Quotations*. Anyway I thought you told me you get seasick?'

'I do. But only in a dinghy – not a big ship like the one I'll be on.'

'There are no rules when it comes to seasickness on board a moving vessel. You chunderers will no doubt be down in your cabins suffering your individual horrors as you count the seconds that make up the minutes that make up the hours.'

Charles shrugged his shoulders and I sighed.

'Oh, one last thing – and I once gave this advice to my son. If you're feeling sick, eat. Eat, eat. Come what may, and come up what may.'

'Huh!' he scoffed. 'That sort of advice is usually given by those who have never suffered anything as normal as nausea, and can stuff their mouths through a force nine gale, then brag about it.'

∴

I dropped my bag next to my desk, straightened my jacket, opened the top drawer and reached for the small pot of royal jelly. Scooping a small amount onto a teaspoon, I swallowed it down with water.

'Hello,' said a voice.

I looked up. I hadn't even noticed that anyone had walked in. Because of the heat, I'd left the door open and the usual chime of warning hadn't sounded.

It turned out to be Mr and Mrs Right.

Yes, Mr and Mrs Right they were. And Mr and Mrs Right they are. Mr Right, who scampered about the neighbourhood as if late for something, and entered places as if he was looking for someone, but in fact really just sniffed for anyone who'd listen to his latest complaints and suspicions, with Mrs Right shuffling along in the background.

'No Charles today?' he asked me.

'No,' I replied. 'He's off on a cruise.'

'Really?'

'Yes, really!'

'Ah, well maybe you can help me. Do you have that biography of the Apple boss? What's his name again? You know, the one that died of cancer. Or was it a heart attack? Anyway, I hear it's rather good.'

I answered with a fixed smile. 'Sold out I'm afraid. I'm expecting a new batch later this morning.'

'Such a genius! I mean where would our lives be without him?' said Mrs Right, and she guffawed with such tooth-white force that I wondered if they were pulling my leg.

'I will put one aside as soon as they arrive.'

Mr Right eyed me with an ice-cube stare. 'Don't bother. I'll try the other shop by the station. They'll definitely have it.'

'Oh yes, bound to. You should have tried them first.'

I knew he loathed me. Why? I wasn't sure. As he always said abrupt things to my face, I wondered what he was capable of saying behind my back. Or does it not work like that?

If people talk to one another openly, are they less likely to gossip in secret? I still haven't found the answer to that one. It's when someone starts talking badly about another that I'm at once suspicious they could do the same about me.

There goes my mind again. Press the stop button.

I thought life would get easier, especially in my head, but I was wrong. The same things exist. All that changes is, they're magnified.

'Why are there so few geniuses these days?' Mr Right asked.

'Much depends on your definition of genius, my darling husband,' chipped in Mrs Right.

'Bugger the definition! I can count today's geniuses on one hand,' moaned Mr Right.

Don't be so despondent, Mr Right, I wanted to say.

Who hasn't heard greatness in the back rows of the orchestra? Haven't we all read letters that match the best literature, or seen magnificent works of art produced by basement dwellers, witnessed actions as kindly as those of saints, or found someone who was funnier at a dinner party than a paid comedian?

The genius is wonderful, but only representative.

I said nothing, though, and let Mrs Right fill the pause.

'We are going next door to the organic restaurant,' she said. 'We just love it there, mixing with the younger people.'

She ever so slightly stressed the word *younger* as if she was hinting at some moral disapprobation, but I recognised my own mind games were in full flow. Maybe it was the heat, or the sense that everything was beginning to drown me.

'Do you ever go there?' she asked.

'Well it is next door, so it would be difficult to avoid," I answered. "But yes, I do. And it's very good. You should try the berry nice smoothie, it's absolutely delicious.'

I smiled.

∴

As the Rights departed, two women walked in. They were an odd pair, and their presence seemed an intrusion. It really is amazing, how some people just annoy the hell out of you. Worryingly for me, it was beginning to happen more and more. The two women started to examine the wide table stacked with the latest publications.

'Let me know if I can help?' I asked, looking up from my desk.

There was silence. They seemed not to have understood. They did not speak the same language as me.

'Let me know if I – can – help - you?' I asked, taking my time over those words.

The younger one, perhaps the daughter, walked over to my desk and peered over my shoulder at the open book I'd been reading. She was straining her eyes like a commuter at someone else's newspaper.

I held the novel up.

'A nice ordinary book taken from a nice ordinary shop,' I said.

The woman stood still, looked at me as if I was mad and made a signal to the older one. She put one hand in front of her face so that her thumb touched the nose, with fingers spread out, and wiggled.

I was sure the action had the same meaning, wherever she came from, as it does here: to express contempt – and, figuratively, show a lack of respect for someone.

Charming!

The elder's hair was long and parted in the middle. The colour was so black, it was blue. She looked at me, pressing her lips together with what I hoped, but could not guarantee, was a smile.

'You give me advice?' she asked.

'I will try.'

'I have pain in stomach.'

'A bad stomach?' I replied, a little confused.

Why would she be telling me the state of her health?

I started a game of charades, circling my stomach with my right hand. There was a brief pause and I saw the woman about to take her chance, presumably expert at exploiting these moments, by pointing to the top shelves.

The top shelves were crammed with a collection of rare first editions.

'I'd go to the pharmacy first if I were you," I said. "Medicine is far better than first editions when it comes to this sort of problem.'

I sensed my voice was unconvincing. Perhaps it was the firm shake of her head.

'Or try next door,' I suggested. 'The mint with dandelion tea is good for a bad stomach.'

The woman again looked confused. Who could blame her? She didn't speak much English and the way I was jumping from one suggestion to another wasn't exactly reassuring. She nodded at her friend, who was standing to my side. She had something of a squint, the sort that has you wondering which of the two eyes is the one looking at you.

'You cannot breathe enough before death,' I thought I heard her mutter.

Whaaaat?

Did she say what I thought she did?

She yawned and stretched. I looked back at the other one, who was at the point of opening *The Rachel Papers*.

'I think you'd like that one.'

The younger one let out a sneeze and I saw particles fall into the open book. I would have usually offered a conciliatory 'Bless you!' but instead, I snapped at her.

'Coughs and sneezes spread diseases!'

The tone of my voice shocked her into dropping Martin Amis on the floor.

I let out a deep sigh and eased myself out of my chair.

She bent down, picked up the book and snapped it closed. 'I'm sorry,' she said, and shoved it into my hands. She then frisked her pockets and looked to her left, right and over my shoulder, acting as if suddenly remembering she'd left something at home.

'Let's go,' she said, signalling to her friend.

The two of them left the shop.

'Next time perhaps, when your health is better, you'll buy something?' I called after them.

I realised they hadn't heard me. They were already scurrying down the street.

I went back to my chair with voices complaining behind me. I didn't like those women. They'd made me feel uneasy.

Why waste your time even talking to people like that?

I was about to reply to myself when I noticed a pile of papers had slipped from my desk. I debated whether or not to bend and pick them up. My lower back had made that simple decision complicated.

How many of us have procrastinated for so long that, by the time we take action, the original reason for that action has evaporated? And we're left standing there, denying vociferously that the action was one we ever intended to take in the first place.

Nevertheless, stooping down, I started to tidy up. Was it my imagination that told my nostrils there was a sour smell when I returned my desk, or told my eyes something was wrong, as if someone had been tampering with my things? I believe that can happen with burglars, when they leave a place in an over-the-top tidy condition, with a load of cushion-pumping and ashtray-emptying likely to be noticeable by the owner and no one else.

Talking of burglars …

Where's my bag?

'I've been robbed!' I cried.

As if right on cue, Colin, my plumber, nonchalantly walked in, shirt tugging at his puffed-up stomach. He was taking a drag from his hand-rolled cigarette and talking incessantly into his mobile phone. After he finished his call, and without drawing breath, he complained.

'How can I keep a family of seven on my wage, with the price of everything going up? Each government worse than the last!'

'Excuse me!' I interrupted.

'Anything wrong?' Colin asked.

'I've been robbed.'

'What?'

'They stole my bag!'

I rushed to the door and looked left, right, left. There was no sign of the two women. I made a half-hearted dash down the street but they were gone.

When I returned to the shop, Colin was puffing away.

'Thanks for your help,' I panted.

'Should I call the police?'

'Yes, why don't you?'

Colin flipped open his mobile phone and started to dial as if he'd called the police many times before. As he did, a thousand thoughts stampeded through my mind.

I was sure something important was in my bag. But what?

'They'll be here in a few minutes.'

'Good,' I said, before thinking out loud, 'I've only been robbed once before.' I looked into Colin's eyes. 'Actually, make that two times.'

He started to roll another cigarette.

'Roll me one!' I ordered.

'I didn't think you smoked.'

'Well I do now.'

We puffed away outside on the street. Colin broke our silence.

'Excuse me, Mr Hammond. This might not be the best time to ask, but was my money in your bag?'

'Money? You mean that exorbitant fee you're charging for the boiler?'

'Er, yes.'

'Yes, all gone!' I replied. 'Every last pound.'

'Oh dear. That's not good,' I heard him mutter.

∴

I knew he was a plain-clothes policeman as soon as I saw him walking towards the shop. If he'd been wearing a raincoat, he might have turned up the lapels in the manner of a screen detective.

He knocked twice on the frame of the open door.

'Come in!' I said with exaggerated composure.

He took a step inside and a sudden breath of air blew in with him.

'Mr Hammond? DC David Brown from Chelsea CID. Has there been a robbery?'

My feigned coolness evaporated. 'Thank you,' I said. 'I mean, no thank you. I mean yes, there has.'

He gave a reassuring smile and looked around the shop like a cricket batsman inspecting the field.

'Let me get some details on what happened,' he said, taking out his pen and notebook.

I was about to reply, as coherently as possible, when the nearby town hall clock struck noon. On most days it could give me a bit of a start, but on this occasion it made me literally jump. Maybe one day I'll remember in time – although waiting for an alarm can be as disquieting as the alarm itself.

The policeman saw my fear and with a voice that was a mix of headmaster, airport announcer and fairground stallholder said, 'Take your time now.'

'I'd like to say how much I appreciate you getting here so quickly.'

'All part of the job, sir.'

I spoke slowly as a single voice throbbed in my head recalling the sequence of events that had just taken place.

'Can you tell me exactly what was taken?'

I answered like a schoolboy reciting his tables. 'A canvas bag with a Union Jack design on it, containing five hundred pounds cash in fifties, a novel by Nathanael West, a small notebook with

some jottings … Shit! It had my house keys … and … and …
Oh, God! A photograph!'

'A photograph?' the policeman queried.

'Yes. A black-and-white one.'

'A black-and-white photograph, you say?'

I nodded.

'Five hundred pounds. Did you say all in fifty-pound notes?'

Again I nodded.

He let out a deep sigh and asked further questions about the
thieves, then more questions I thought I'd already given answers
to. He asked them at a pace not dissimilar to the speed at which
a boxer fires jabs at his opponent. The only problem was, I
thought we were on the same side.

'What's the likelihood of finding the photograph?' I asked,
between breaths. Now, nothing else mattered. I coughed to clear
my dry throat as if simply asking the question had tightened it.

'To be frank, sir – and if a man isn't frank, what can he be? –
but these thieves will only be interested in the cash. They're not
interested in anything else. Around here, they usually throw the
bag and all the other stuff into the Thames,' he replied.

His answer winded me. I could hardly find the air to breathe.

The policeman sucked in his waist and tucked his notebook
away into his jacket. He made no recognition that I was in pain.

That casual remark of his, about it being unlikely anything
would be found, felt like broken glass piercing me. Before
leaving, he bemoaned the passing of the good old days when
people could be trusted and front doors could be left unlocked.
His eyes were those of an old dog, the twinkle diminished

years ago.

'I'd better be going. No time to lose as they say.'

I collapsed into my chair and another conversation started in my head.

Look what age does: you lose your closest friends and replace them with imaginary ones.

'Excuse me, sir, one more question …'

The policeman had made a quick return.

'… Just before I start my enquiries, what was the photograph of?'

II

Five days before Christmas.

I can't claim to be one of those who pull back the curtains and shout with joy at another day but, once awake, I am fully awake. A sign of a good night or a troubled conscience? I haven't forgotten anything from that day in December 1988, not even lying with my head propped up by two pillows, in a sort of meditation, thinking that in the New Year I might finally break free from working in the City of London and change career.

Ah, that would be something! How does that quote go?

Fear knocked at the door. Faith opened. And there was no one there.

The hot water wasn't working. A December morning and no hot water, no problem – especially after suffering the indignity of those early morning showers at boarding school, where one had to suffer the chill 'without murmur, without sound.'

I put my head under the cold water and had a quick shave with an extra dollop of soap. Shaving is better with hot water, and I almost cut myself with my razor on the rim of my nostril – always a bad place to draw blood, adding at least ten minutes to your journey into the office.

I slapped on my more expensive lemon-smelling aftershave, which I tended to reserve for special occasions or thoughts. I wiped away a smidgen of foam from behind one ear and walked downstairs to the kitchen to have my daily fix of caffeine.

The silence was golden – or should I say plain yellow, because just as I was thinking how peaceful everything was, the morning post dropped through the letterbox.

The coffee tasted good, so much so that I treated myself to another cup, firmly against my normal rules. But it was Christmas week, after all. I was in no rush. The stock markets had slowed and the days were full of partying rather than buying or selling shares. I would take the morning easy, let myself into the rhythm of the day, smell the coffee.

I picked up the post and was carrying it to the kitchen table when a brown envelope suddenly fell away from the others, apparently of its own accord or perhaps pushed by a poltergeist. When we bought the house, a neighbour had suggested a ghost would share our lives. My wife Kate and I laughed it off. We were more charmed by the prospect of living with a piece of history.

'I bet it's Anne Boleyn,' Kate had said, and we laughed at the absurdity of it all. Or perhaps we were laughing because we were gloriously happy about moving into our first home.

The envelope made a slapping sound as it landed on the kitchen tiles. I bent down and picked it up. On the back a red-inked stamp bore the words Horizon Travel.

Ah, what a relief! My son's airline ticket had arrived, just in the nick of time. I was treating him to a business class return to New York for his Christmas present. He'd fallen madly in love with a girl on the other side of the Atlantic. He'd said he felt guilty about leaving me at Christmas, nervously questioning whether I would be okay. Of course I'd be okay, I told him. And how was I to argue, anyway? I could hardly complain that he was newly experiencing the joy of a true love and discovering the real purpose of life – maybe even preparing to start a new life.

The plane was due to leave Heathrow the following evening at six. I understood the rule to be no ticket, no travel – but I may have been wrong. Anyway, the mini-drama of talking to the travel agent and their promise that 'it was sent a week ago' were now over.

Luke could travel safely and without concern.

I was about to open the envelope there and then, but for some reason decided I would keep it for later when I had dealt with the more mundane post. I set it on the edge of the table, much as someone might place the best morsel on the side of the plate to keep it for the very end of the meal.

Around a third of the post proved to be Christmas cards, from people I hadn't heard from or spoken to in years. The majority of items were special offers for summer holidays, most of which were soon torn to shreds and strewn across the table like discarded betting slips. One I did keep, mainly because of its accidental humour: a leaflet advertising a summer cruise. *Book early to avoid disappointment* was the headline, followed by a list of countries it would visit, ending with a peculiar warning about being careful not to fall overboard. Pessimistic or what?

Do not try to swim, the last paragraph warned. *Lie on your back. Save energy. You should be able to do this for twenty-four hours. The ship will eventually turn to find you.*

Perhaps this was a lesson about life: don't flap, have faith, you're always in with a chance of rescue. How reassuring! And, just below the paragraph, was the request for a deposit.

I sat up with a jolt. The phone had rung. Back then I still had one of those lovely old handsets with a proper bell.

'Hello.'

'Yes?'

'Hello?'

I paused.

'Daddy, it's Luke!'

I laughed and said, 'I know it's you, silly. I was just expecting someone else.'

Now it was his turn to laugh. 'Anyone I should know?'

'Not really. I'll tell you later.'

We'd been invited to a charity do later that evening. Something about keeping the little zoo in the local park open. When I say zoo, I don't mean lions and tigers, more like donkeys and peacocks. Even so, close to Christmas it was a sell-out. I presumed that some of the locals found it hard to turn down the invitation. One positive thing about giving to something near you, something you could quite possibly see every day, is it cancels out that time-worn excuse of refusing to give to charity because 'there's no guarantee it'll get to where it's supposed to'.

'Don't forget it's black tie tonight,' I said.

'Let's take a taxi. I want us to get really drunk tonight. Get into the Christmas spirit so to speak,' Luke said.

'That sounds fun but make sure you don't mix your drinks.'

'Dad, please!' Luke replied, in a certain tone he'd used for as long as I could remember.

'Oh, before I forget, your airline ticket has arrived. The panic is over ... I'll bring them over later.'

I reached for the envelope while talking and started to pull out the airline ticket.

'No, you look after them. You're still taking me to the airport tomorrow, aren't you?'

Of course I was. I tucked the ticket back in its envelope and shoved it briskly under the cruise leaflet, like a secret agent disturbed while photographing an enemy report.

'You try to stop me. I'm taking the whole day off work tomorrow.'

'Great.'

'Oh, here's a thing. You don't want to take your girlfriend on a cruise, do you? I just received this rather bizarre leaflet advertising a summer cruise with a footnote advising how to survive if you accidentally fall overboard.'

I read through each point as if I were standing in a pulpit.

'It sounds as useful as when you told me what do when chased by a bull.'

'But you were going to Spain,' I replied.

'I was spending a week at the Marbella Club! What did you say again? Oh yes!' Luke began to imitate my voice. 'If being chased by a bull one should lie down in the middle of the field and pretend one is dead or, if that doesn't work, divert their short-sighted attention by throwing something in one direction and then run like hell in the other. Jesus, if that's not a contradiction I don't know what is.'

I tried to interrupt but there was no stopping him.

'What about the time I visited Kenya and you advised me, if I were bitten by a snake, not to panic as this increases the beat of one's heart and therefore the speed at which the venom is pumped round the body? Also, not to forget to kill the snake and take it to the hospital, so the doctors know which serum to give you ... I mean, really, Dad!'

'I was only trying to be helpful.'

'I know,' he said lovingly. And I felt the warmth glide down the phone.

I finished the call with, 'I've got to be going. I'll see you tonight: seven o'clock sharp!'

∴

It took me four years to paint like Raphael, but a lifetime to paint like a child. As I walked towards the tube station, I thought of those pertinent words by Picasso. Let's try to erase the cluttered; I knew I needed change. I had to start to get things done, to get a move on. Much of what happened in those days was like a cloud that, like the moment itself, soon changes, passes and is never to be repeated.

As I breathed in the cold morning air, I decided in the coming months I'd quit my job and do what I really needed to do.

'What lies ahead?' I spoke out loud.

'No one knows. Just remember problems are always less difficult than you dread them to be,' a stranger said, clearly overhearing me.

I looked at this wire-haired man who stopped, took out a pipe and a pouch from his blazer pocket and, pressing some tobacco down into the bowl with a thumb, extricated a match from a matchbox, lit the match and then the tobacco all with one hand, turned, smiled at me like an old sailor in one of those frozen fish advertisements and wished me a cheerful farewell.

I paid for my ticket and waited for the train. By the size of the crowd I could tell the wait had already been too long. How I wanted my liberty: to skim, to survive, to arrive. To create that chance so that everywhere is somewhere to reach. To be happy knowing that the only thing of which we can be sure is the next heartbeat.

The only real question we can ask ourselves is just how many times will we breathe this breath, step this spot, and write this word? That's what I was thinking that December Tuesday, standing on the roofless platform shadowed by the early morning grey sky.

∴

The previous evening had been my office Christmas party and my secretary had got tipsy, or should I say plastered. Miss Varley had crossed that invisible line into vagueness and vitriol. I noticed Mr Lloyd, one of the traders, was trying to take full advantage of the situation, hoping to get a favour that on a sober day would have been impossible.

Everything is possible if you strike at the right moment.

At one point, Miss Varley swayed uneasily over and said, 'I'm not a whore, you know.'

What was she talking about? I never thought she was. Although I admit I did have a secret fantasy about having an office affair with her, I'd resisted, the old adage being to never shit on your own doorstep.

'Poor creature,' I thought I heard someone say.

Others nodded their agreement.

Another said, 'Those who can't face life should be forced to pull themselves together or seek help.'

'Or at least stay clear of the rest of us,' said someone else.

'Why don't you stay clear of us, then?' another added aggressively.

'Why, you ...!'

A row, fight, even a battle, threatened to break out. It doesn't take much to get some people wound up.

When I turned away from the potential scrap, Miss Varley was pouring more wine into Mr Lloyd's glass. He paused, smelled it and was about to take a sip, as if at the altar rail, when she grabbed the glass and refused to hand it back.

She glanced over to check I was watching.

Mr Lloyd frowned but said simply, 'Don't worry. Let's use another one!'

He picked up a clean glass from the table and held it in Miss Varley's direction to be filled. She hesitated, let out a sozzled laugh and eventually poured out a little of the wine, shrugging her shoulders as if to suggest what will be, will be.

All was calm for a moment but in the time it took me to move to the other side of the room, the wine had been spilled onto Mr Lloyd's suit and Miss Varley had collapsed to the floor. Mr Lloyd moved as if to help her. She brushed him away, as if to say that he was already too late and, in any case, as he had no true intention of helping her, he should not make a belated pretence.

She dusted down her long grey dress and shuffled off in my direction. As she headed towards me, I couldn't help but hear her whimpering. The noise passed through many stages until reaching a crescendo: tittering, giggling, gurgling, gargling, laughing, and guffawing – until, at the top of her voice, she started to cheer.

It was time to come to Miss Varley's rescue. As my father had once told me, 'when people have drunk too much, just place a blanket over them and let them sleep.'

He was right. Is there anything quite so nice as having a blanket put over you when you're tired and inebriated?

'Miss Varley, I think you need to get home, don't you? Let's call you a taxi.'

'I'm sorry. I'm so sorry. You're the last person in the world I would want to embarrass.'

And, quite uncontrollably, she started to weep.

I ordered the taxi driver to take her straight home. 'Make sure she's safe,' I said, handing him the fare.

As the taxi began to move away, she wound down the window and shouted out into the cold night, 'Why don't you ever call me?'

∴

I walked into the office as Miss Varley was calmly pulling out a sheet of paper from the typewriter. It was a short, well-written resignation letter, which she laid on her desk.

Picking it up, I asked her to follow me into my office.

'Sit down, Miss Varley.'

I looked at her rather beautiful face made even more so because of her vulnerability. Embarrassed, she shuffled and played with the hem of her navy blue dress.

Her eyes said, 'I am very sorry and feel foolish.'

She started to cry.

'Hey, stop that,' I said, handing her a clean handkerchief from my pocket, with which she dabbed her blue eyes. 'Let's move on. There are a lot worse things than getting drunk at the office party. Ask the insane, the terminally ill, or the battered wife trying to control their drink!'

Her face dropped.

'I'm sorry," I said. 'That was a silly thing to say. What I really mean is, the show must go on. Mustn't it? Well … Technically speaking, it doesn't have to, I suppose, but we can be almost certain it will, in some shape or form, so we might as well say that it must, preferably in the shape or form we most want it … Is that clear? No? Yes? Good! Now go wipe your eyes. And stop worrying.'

She looked unsure.

'Valerie, I said don't worry,' I reiterated. 'Everything will be all right.'

She stood up, almost gave a curtsey and left my office.

∴

I glanced at the company's annual report and took notes of one or two, maybe three or four, even fourteen, forty, relevant sentences for my department. I did it in a matter-of-fact, dispassionate manner. I then dropped the thin, green file onto a junior's desk. I asked him to arrange for copies to be distributed by hand or post, or even faxed to clients around the globe.

'Make sure you give it a read over the Christmas break, it will give you a good overview on the company,' I said, in a paternal tone, to the gawky young man who wore glasses the size of plates.

He'd no doubt try to read the damn thing but be very unlikely to get beyond page two. He might attempt to browse through the rest when he had nothing better to do, but almost certainly wouldn't be able to take it all in. The report is dull. Was dull. Would be forever dull. I bet most of the copies around the world would find their way into shredders, wastepaper baskets, and rubbish bins.

∴

The phone was ringing when I returned to my office.

'Hello!'

It was Luke, asking if I wanted to join him for lunch.

'I am sorry, I can't get away.'

'No problem. I'm meeting some friends. I was just wondering if you were around.'

'Okay. See you tonight.'

It was a conversation no more than the length of those sentences, slowly diminishing into the ether: short, missing the exact moment of its significance but it was a conversation, is a conversation, that has stayed in my mind for years.

As I put the telephone down, Miss Varley walked in. Her eyes were now clear.

'Can I get you anything?'

'I don't think so. I'm just going out to buy Luke a sweater. It gets cold in New York this time of the year; knowing him, he won't have packed enough warm clothes.'

'You're a good father you know, and he's a lovely boy. I'll never forget you telling me what he said to you when he heard the news of his mother's death.'

I shook my head. For one instant there was true silence: that near-true nothing sought after by audio purists, poets and meditators.

'Sorry, have I overstepped the mark again?'

I shook my head again.

It was eleven years ago. I couldn't remember telling Miss Varley about that day but I suppose I must have.

∴

The soul has no age and, as I was once told, the age of a human being shouldn't necessarily be calculated from the moment of birth but from the time at which the human starts to live honestly.

For Luke, that time started in the womb.

∴

When I was a student at Oxford, I lived opposite a musician who would practice from dusk to dawn. At night, I would listen from my bed to the vintage tones of her grand piano. Sometimes she'd leave her window open and I'd hear more clearly the mad merry dance. Or was it a war between the hammers and wires?

For nearly a term, I didn't meet my neighbour. My housemate had told me how beautiful she was and that she'd taken up teaching the piano to pay her rent.

'I want to learn how to play piano with her,' he enthused. 'Some deliciously corny repeatable tunes, like *Night and Day*.'

So, he took up classes in the flat opposite. Or so I thought. When I asked him how it was going, he said in a huff that it wasn't. His piano teacher didn't date her students – especially those who asked her out during their first lesson.

Although I remember laughing and probably thinking that was my type of girl, I didn't give it another thought because I was dating an Irish girl who occupied my spare time both physically and mentally. But then came the day I watched this beautiful creature cycling down our road.

My eyes followed her to the house opposite. I immediately knew who she must be. The very next day, I took up the piano.

My teacher's name was Kate. Kate Lowther.

I married Kate six months after we first met. I proposed to her in the middle of one of my classes and my housemate was my best man.

This isn't Kate's story but, when I talk of Luke, I feel her presence.

So much of Kate was similar to Luke. All corny but true. He had his mother's green eyes, her hair the colour of Peruvian brown. How their smiles would linger long after the laughter. Most of all, they shared that sensitivity, which touched everyone they encountered.

All of us are made up from aspects of family. What do they say? If you don't know where you came from, you won't know where you're going. Better to say, let's try to commemorate them – for how many of us know the names, let alone the life stories or characters of even our great-grandparents?

Although Kate had been sick for some time – two years to be exact – there was no indication she would die that Monday morning.

'Sick people take hostages,' she said, whispering the pitiful words. Soon after, she closed her eyes and never regained consciousness.

I escaped the house as soon as I could. I yearned to be my son's side.

'I'll keep the news to myself,' the headmaster of his prep school blithely said. 'We do think it works better coming from a family member.'

It was a two-hour car journey to Kent. Over the river, across South London, red lights greeted me on every block. I stared out, hands tight on the wheel, rehearsing what I was going to say to Luke. I planned to look straight into his eyes and not for one moment turn away, even if the pain of seeing the sorrow etched on his face became unbearable.

I gripped the driving wheel as if to gather my strength.

'Come on!'

As I drove through the suburbs, the first bleak thoughts of grief spluttered and eventually gushed over me. How suddenly life can truly change. Yet I didn't weep on the journey, even though I knew nothing would ever be the same again. My mouth was dry, my eyes felt parched and I was thirsty, but I kept on driving. I was incapable of concentrating on a single thought long enough to make decisions, let alone read road signs. At times, I didn't know where I was, fumbling for music on the radio and, in the process, missing my turn, needing to double back to get onto the right road again.

I groaned, moaned and bemoaned at regular intervals.

'If only … only only … only only only …'

I indulged in the blame game: perhaps I could have done more, found a better doctor, taken her to America where they had better clinics, taken Luke out of school to spend more days with his mother?

The grotesque guilt at first flickered and flashed in my mind like fireflies, or camera bulbs flashing in a night- time stadium: lights going on and off, signifying people being born and dying around the globe. And then it began to dazzle me, like a sunset shining through a break in darkened clouds, finally blinding me like searchlights shining straight into my eyes.

Whatever I knew about guilt – that it was, in fact, a purposeless pastime that sucked the blood out of the soul, and sent you deeper into a trough of self-concern – I still couldn't stop myself.

I reached the Kent coast. I opened the car window to breathe in the English sea air. I could hear the sound of gulls returning to shore after a long-distance hunt into the wilds of the North Sea. They tend to follow the ships, gliding above, aloof until, suddenly, they plunge *en masse* with a squawk and screech towards the remnants of meals, chucked overboard.

Seagulls, I've been told, are the souls of dead sailors.

And what, pray, happens to the souls of the rest of us?

Then, quickly, my mood changed. I began to feel the start of that delicious tingling in in the head that usually comes from the perfect blend of peace of mind, a slight current of air and an unexpected small act of kindness on the part of someone else.

It was beautiful, and I believed my late wife had sent her love to help me through those last, late miles until I reached the school.

When I arrived, the school grounds were deserted. There were no nets on the goal posts and the swimming pool was covered. There was an eerie sense of solitude as I made my way to the headmaster's office.

'Come in,' the headmaster said, in a tone that gave me the impression it had been rehearsed for ages, in order to make his voice more refined than it really was.

'How do you do,' he said in a self-satisfied, hearty fashion.

'Good trip down?'

Oh yes, headmaster, thank you.

'I'll get him for you,' he said, picking up his phone.

'Let him finish his lesson first. I don't want him dragged out of class in front of all his friends. I think that would be unkind, don't you?'

The headmaster paused and said, 'Quite so, quite so.'

And we sat facing each other in one of the quietest silences I had ever heard. I mean, quieter than any examination hall or library, early morning bus, changing room of a losing (or worse, relegated) team, place of worship or listening submarine.

'Won't be long now,' the headmaster said.

I nodded. Time was moving slowly and that was my excuse for a plethora of examples of silence: here I was, waiting for my son to tell him his mother had died, and I was making a list.

The headmaster coughed loudly out of nowhere. To clear a dry throat like the one I had, or warn me that the bell was about to ring? Indeed, it did, loudly – very loudly – followed by a cacophony of trampling feet and high-pitched voices.

I jumped out of my skin.

'I'll go and get him and will leave you two alone.'

I sat there without reply, gormlessly staring into space. While I waited those long, long minutes, I spoke out loud a prayer for the dead.

Everyone loved her.
She was part of the sun.
Now she is spared the cruelties and crimes of this mortal life,
and can return to the sun to which she belongs.
Everyone loved her.
For us that sun is a little duller today,
though it will brighten on the morrow.

I shivered. I heard the sound of a voice. Was that Luke's? I shivered again. No. So I looked down. I looked again. I strained my eyes. I tried to do the right thing. I made a wish.

Oh, I wish I didn't have to be saying what I'm about to say. That life was different.

I wait, I am waiting, will wait, will be waiting, waited, have waited, have been waiting, had waited, had been waiting, will have waited, will have been waiting ...

And then *whoosh!* – the door opened and my son was standing there, eleven years old in school uniform, there in front of me, looking straight into my eyes.

'Your mother died this morning.'

I said five words. I just said them.

'Your mother died this morning.'

I held out my arms and I hugged my son. My beautiful, beautiful son.

Here I am, here I was, here I am.

I heard my son's cry. No hate, no blame. This is our story and we must deal with it together. At least we have each other.

'Go and pack, Luke. I'm going to take you home.'

'And I won't be coming back here, will I, Daddy?'

'You won't?'

'No! We have to look after each other now,' so said my eleven-year-old son, and he said it with a kind of urgency that told me he believed we should try to spend every day together.

When he left the room, I finally broke down.

∴

I had not seen her. I was sure I had not seen her. It was obviously a trick of my imagination.

I felt her presence around the house.

Like so many people in mourning, Luke seemed to be trying to make amends. Somehow he felt guilty, blamed himself for her death. Why, I will never know. I could pretend to be a leading psychiatrist and try to explain, have an answer for Luke's innermost feelings during that first year following on from Kate's death, but I can't.

All I do know is, the house was consumed by silence. Rarely did Luke lift his eyes to meet mine. If only I could've found the words to say in those few months, to tell him it was no one's fault, that life is given and taken away, inexplicably. But I couldn't. I couldn't even look after myself, and felt ashamed that I wasn't being the father I had hoped to be.

I quickly found a place for him at a prep school in North London.

'How very lucky,' friends would say, 'it is so difficult to get in there.'

It wasn't luck at all. I knew the chairman of the governors, who had dated Kate as a teenager.

'I kissed her all night,' he curiously admitted during our phone call.

Aren't people strange?

'How lovely,' I replied.

Luke found comfort in ordinary things, like playing a game of football on a Saturday afternoon: ordinary days, ordinarily passing, full of their ordinary, fine things and ordinary woes – life's ups, downs and levelling off.

'Are you okay?' I'd ask.

'I'm okay,' he'd reply.

And I'd leave it there. Too scared to ask follow-up questions, many of which I'd rehearse at four o'clock on most mornings. It was about the same time when Luke crept into my bedroom one Sunday.

'Are you awake, Dad?' he asked.

'Yes,' I whispered.

'You know what next Friday is?'

I grabbed his hand. I knew.

'It's a year since Mum died. Can we go to her grave and say hello to her?'

'Of course. Of course we can.'

Luke leaned down and gave me a deep hug. It was my first hug in many months. I understood in that moment that maybe, and I repeat maybe, he just didn't want to get too close since his mother died. The pain of losing one parent is too devastating to risk the thought of losing another. Keep your distance, it'll help. I could've been wrong but something told me it was true when I felt his warm breath close to my neck.

The night before our visit to the cemetery, after Luke had gone to bed, I opened a bottle of wine to keep me company. Company? Wine was my best friend in those days. Wine helped me to wash away the hours I knew I'd have been sharing with Kate if she'd still been alive. I drank to soak up the pain. Does that make sense?

The morning of Kate's anniversary, my head was throbbing. The extra bottle of wine might've been excessive. I looked in the mirror and thought I might be sick at any moment. I sat on the edge of the bath, waiting for the room to return to stability. I thought for a moment that today, of all days, I wished I had a clear head – no whirlwind of the eyes, no throb, no dryness of the tongue.

I picked myself up, literally placing my hands under my bottom. I walked into the kitchen to exorcise the previous night's intake. I saw one bottle of wine with still enough left in it for a morning slurp. I poured it into a fresh glass and regretted it instantly because I would have to clean it, before our housekeeper Lidia arrived and caught my sneaky retreat into drink.

I think Lidia was starting to suspect my late-night habit had become more than just a habit. The previous week I was sure I heard a *tut-tut* as we passed each other on the stairs.

I wanted to say, 'Don't judge me, Lidia,' but in truth she was right.

I needed to change.

I stood at my son's bedroom door looking at him. He was asleep, still in a deep dream. I saw one leg shake intermittently, the summer morning still grey, the knot on brow tied tightly.

The night before surged from both ends of my spectrum of sense: one minute near to tears of joy, the next closer to tears of anguish.

I went to switch on the kettle but instead I opened the cupboard next to the cooker, pulling out a bottle of brandy. I poured, the neck of the bottle rattling against the glass. I drank the wine in one swig, like swallowing medicine as a child. Nothing changed; the separation was evident, refused to shift.

Looking for a cigarette I hoped would help, I found a crumpled packet of Marlboros had fallen onto the floor below the kitchen table. I lit one up and inhaled a deep drag. The brandy had begun to numb me, the unearthly hour of the morning becoming more bearable as a consequence. I stood and paced over to the kettle, relieved to find it was full of water. I hated having to fill it up. I pressed the red switch and waited for the water to boil. The intensity of the day was so unmistakable, my damn head still throbbing.

Won't anything work?

I popped an aspirin into a glass of water and hoped it would do some good. As I swallowed, the sun came up, shining directly into my eyes and giving me a lithium shot.

It was going to be a warm day. I decided to shave before I woke Luke up. Best he slept a little longer. Twelve years old and he could still sleep, whatever the day promised.

I needed to be strong. Strong for both of us. I had to be the father I knew I could, would, be.

I felt the coarseness of my beard growth. I didn't want to be unshaven. Seeing someone unshaved always gave me a sense of mourning. I squeezed too much foam onto my face. I wiped half of it off and started, in a meditative state, to shape the remainder into a thick white beard.

So this is how I'll look in the coming years.

I examined my eyes in the mirror. And what eyes!

My hair wet from the splash of water, I shaved carefully and precisely. I cut against the edges, which usually drew blood, but not that day. I leaned over the sink and splashed warm water over my face.

It was the perfect shave. That was something.

I slapped aftershave over my chin and neck. It was the same aftershave Kate gave me for my birthday, two years before. It sunk into my face and just as I was letting out a deep sigh, I heard Lidia arrive with a slam of the front door.

I hurried to Luke's room. He was lying in the exact same position as earlier but snoring a little louder.

'Luke, darling. It's time to get up.'

He let out the widest of yawns and immediately smiled as if he was looking forward to sharing the day.

'Are you okay?' I asked.

'Yes I'm fine,' he answered with another yawn.

∴

We hailed a taxi outside the tube station. It had been a bad summer for taxis, no rain but a storm of inflation.

'Where to, guv?'

'Highgate. The cemetery.'

The drive was interspersed with chat about how badly our football team played last season.

'Better next year, what do you think, guv?'

'Yes, better next year,' I replied not thinking, not interested.

But Luke was having none of it. He was keen to pursue the conversation and test the driver's football knowledge.

As we pulled up to the cemetery, the two of them were laughing over a player's laziness in running back to defend for his team.

'They should sell him!' Luke said, and the cab driver guffawed in agreement.

We had found the perfect ride to distract us from the coming hour.

As we walked towards the plot, I started to weep far more than I had on the day of the funeral, when we had been surrounded by anguish and cries of pain. The suffering from the clustered grouping had been overwhelming. My only consolation had been ordinary hugs from relative strangers, whispering their 'I am terribly sorry' words of comfort.

'Your mother had the most beautiful smile,' I suddenly said.

Luke said nothing but smiled just like his mother used to.

I recited some words. The same words I said to myself when I waited to break the news to Luke.

Everyone loved her. She was part of the sun …

We didn't stay long. We didn't want to stare at a tombstone that read *Kate Hammond, Beloved Wife and Mother*. The simplicity of the epitaph made the whole damn waste, the tragedy of life, seemingly fit. It didn't need a description of personality: generous, warm, kind, a mother so passionate for life and always so … happy.

And then Luke said something I found strange.

'I never saw her cry,' he said.

'Didn't she cry when we dropped you off at prep school?'

And he shook his head.

But she did, I remembered.

Kate had looked down at Luke with a gravity that made her face so very beautiful. She'd taken a deep breath and her tearful eyes had creased.

'It won't be long, darling, before you're back with us in London,' she said. I want you to promise that you'll be brave. Promise me now …'

And she had knelt, and I know he must have smelled her skin. Her skin, with the scent of freshly sliced apples.

As we walked away from the cemetery up the hill, our silence was broken by the scream of an ambulance speeding by, followed by another and another. Three altogether.

Oh dear, I thought.

At the same time, Luke turned to me. 'I've never seen that before,' he said. 'Two, perhaps. But three? That can't be good.'

I felt his hand grab my sleeve, reaching for reassurance. As I felt my shirt being tugged, I thought, *I'll always keep you safe, my son.* I should have said it out loud – but, like so many things when you reflect back on your life, I didn't.

'Shall we go in?' he asked, as we walked past a rural-looking pub with tables outside.

I answered with a smile and led him in through a small oak door.

A man was propped against the bar, gazing down into his near-empty glass. 'It can't be that bad,' I wanted to say. We gave each other a nod: a 'so you come to the pub early as well' sort of greeting.

The pub was surprisingly full. It must have been just past midday. An old lady sat at a small table, drinking her gin and tonic deliberately and when she caught the eye of the man propping up the bar, she lifted her nose as if trying to avoid a bad smell.

One alcoholic judging another.

'A Coca-Cola …' I asked and then paused before saying, 'One for me as well, please.'

No more drinking. No more excuses. I had to look after Luke and not spend my time wallowing in self-pity.

'Father and son?' the pub landlord asked with the smirk of an over-friendly cop.

'Yes,' Luke replied proudly.

We walked outside with our drinks and packets of salt and vinegar crisps. We sat at a table next to a young family celebrating a birthday. The father had received a camera from his wife, and was very happy. It was a Leica – well, at least that's what it said on the box – and he handled it gently. He asked an old man shuffling from table to table whether he would mind shooting a family snap. The man had been begging, so this was his chance to earn some cash.

Snap!

He was duly paid, earning his fifty pence with a minimal amount of work.

The weather was handing out a soporific mood, with many of those gathered at the pub looking half-asleep, with their mouths slightly open. Luke let out another of his yawns and covered his mouth with his right hand.

'Sorry,' he said.

'Your mother would have liked it here.'

'What do you think she'd be drinking?' Luke asked.

'Probably a glass of white wine.'

'Would you go and buy her one?'

I paused and said, 'Of course I will.'

And so I went in and bought my late wife a glass of wine, putting it down in front of an empty seat.

Luke frowned. 'There's so much I don't know about her,' he said. 'It's funny how, until you lose someone, you don't think about it, do you?'

'Ask me,' I said. 'Ask me anything you want.'

Life is one long 'if only.' But it wasn't on that warm afternoon. I answered everything he wanted to know: from when Kate and I had first kissed (Bardwell Road, Oxford) to who chose the name Luke (she did), to what her favourite colour was (blue).

Luke spoke more softly than I'd ever heard him before, leaning forward to tell me he how felt those first few months after she died, how he thought of when she smiled, how he heard her voice calling out, 'Dinner's ready!'

And he let out a laugh as he remembered how his mum always got cross that I was late to the table for dinner.

'Don't all wives do that?'

'I don't know. I've never been married but when I am, I'll let you know.'

I was happy to hear his humour again. I'd spent so long imagining his dark thoughts when I caught him sometimes looking out onto the street, quite still and silent, his head reflected in windows: a thousand angles, telling a thousand stories.

Have we got a cure for dying?
Can anyone truly be trained in God?
Is Luke's mother watching us from that crow's nest in the sky?

From that afternoon on, we spoke openly with each other. Even the early teenage years you'd imagine would be difficult, they weren't. They sped by without drama. Luke passed his common entrance exam to a London day school. There was never any debate as to whether he'd be going back to boarding. No, we spent time together and, although he encouraged me to go out and meet someone, I never took any of my dates seriously. My attention was focused on bringing up my son. I didn't have room for anyone else.

I was about to ask whether Luke wanted another Coke, when a woman at another table fell off her chair. We turned to see her pushing herself up off the ground with one of her arms.

'Time to go,' I suggested.

As we walked away from Highgate, the rain started to fall, with such strength we both thought Kate had ordered it for our entertainment. A loving couple holding hands skipped between the puddles that were quickly forming, now and again having to let go as they jumped in different directions. A man waiting for a bus with his shirt collar pulled up visibly paled in front of my eyes, like a schoolboy smoking his first illicit cigarette. I was just thinking someone should help him when he darted to a nearby house for cover.

Luke stood still, looking up into the rain. I watched as it lashed against his face, now past the point of showing concern that we were both getting drenched. I noticed his hands as he ran them across his face, his cut fingernails a little dirty from the soil of his mother's grave.

The rain on his face made it difficult for me to tell if he was crying. Everything seemed to be moving in slow motion until, just as I thought the magnificence of the storm would last for a month, the rain stopped and the sun reappeared like a magic trick. I watched it buffet and bash one large and dark cloud, pressing it to move away towards Kenwood house.

Luke looked into my eyes. 'Shall we get home?'

'Yes, let's go home,' I replied.

We walked past the Hampstead Ponds holding each other's hands, drying off in the now warm afternoon sunshine.

∴

Bishopsgate was packed with Christmas shoppers. I needed to get the hell out of there, needed to get away from the crowd.

I headed into the first men's store. I was in luck. The finest cashmere from the Highlands of Scotland. The shop assistant was talking to a small man with a nasal voice, who was clearly pretending to be lost only in order to hold a conversation with someone ... or anyone.

'Can we hurry this up?' I said rather too loudly.

They looked round and continued to talk.

I was impatient that morning, as if I knew I should be elsewhere. 'Calm down,' I said to myself. 'Look in a mirror and give yourself a wink,' which is exactly what I did and miraculously for a moment it did indeed calm me.

'I'm looking for a sweater.'

'V neck or crew?'

'I'm not sure. It's for my son who's off to New York. I think crew – no V – no, crew. What about a polo neck?'

Decisions. Indecision. Actions. Inaction. In the end, we settled on a navy blue polo neck.

'That should keep your son warm,' said the assistant. 'New York can be bitterly cold at this time of the year. I know, I used to live there.'

'No need to wrap it, just put it in the bag,' I said.

'Would you like the receipt?'

'No, thank you.'

I picked the bag up and walked out.

The supposedly best restaurant in the City was busy – and I mean, very busy. Marco, the maître d, stood guard at the swing doors. He was begging those outside not to move inside until those inside had moved outside, and those inside he was pressing to hurry up and move outside. But those moving outside were having substantial difficulty in making their way through.

I saw the bar area, rocking with laughter. The noise was nearly overwhelming but I was hungry, Marco was always accommodating, and it was evident that to get a table, a certain amount of favouritism was involved. He beckoned me with his eyes and, before anyone had noticed, I was already at my table and ordering lunch.

Marco was asking everyone to calm down, assuring them there was no point in shoving.

'The food is not going to run away!' he joked.

'Well, where is my bloody food, then?' the man on the next table demanded. He was red in the face. So red, in fact, it was clear this was only the latest in a long line of blood-pressure-raising problems.

He looked sad and angry but I may have been wrong.

'Excuse me, sir,' a waiter said. And, with a smile that was as forced as it was wide, he offered me a wicker basket in which lay a bottle of wine, with its head and neck protruding from a white napkin.

It was as if he were introducing me to a baby, wrapped up warm in its cradle.

'A Christmas gift from Marco.'

I looked at the bottle. At Marco. Back at the bottle.

'Thank you, Marco!' I mouthed. 'Uncork it, please.'

'A fine wine, sir!'

The waiter started to pour, his moustache twitching.

I smiled to myself, probably my first smile of the day. The uneasiness began to fade. I picked myself up, dusted myself down, and decided to start the day all over again. I sipped my wine and enjoyed it – so much so, I kicked the white tablecloth that reached down towards the floor. I moved instinctively to check for my shopping bag, which I'd set at my side under the table.

'Where's my bag?' I blurted out.

I felt a shudder up my spine. It had been stolen.

Wait a moment – who was that heading for the swing doors? *'Hey, you! Stop!'*

The man was on the street before I barged my way outside.

There he was, bouncing up and down, weaving in and out of the crowd.

I chased him, yelling '*Stop that man!*' and eventually catching the thief, just, by grabbing the tail of his shirt. He struggled free of me only by ripping his shirt, in a way not unlike an armadillo, which sheds its tail when caught.

A silence rippled across the shoppers and a face looked down at me with an expression I can only describe as pregnant.

The woman put a hand on my shoulder and said, 'I think this must be yours.'

It was my shopping bag. With the polo neck sweater safe inside.

'Thank you! In fact, it's really for my son,' I said, calmly dusting myself down.

The chase had lifted my spirits.

As I sat back down in the restaurant, the man with the red face leaned forward, an elbow on the table, his head cupped in one hand and his glass in the other.

'I want to know if I guessed correctly,' he asked drunkenly. 'You let him go, didn't you?'

'Yes. I suppose I did,' I replied.

'Why?'

'I don't know. Perhaps because he was too strong for me. Or maybe because it's Christmas.'

'Huh! Damn Christmas. Those bastards should be locked up. Castrated!'

I didn't wait for the waiter. Instead, I dropped some money on the table that would more than cover the food.

I left the restaurant somehow knowing I would never return.

∴

The temperature had suddenly dropped. With a darkening grey sky, I wasn't sure if it was about to rain or snow.

'Taxi!' I yelled.

Too bored to go back to the office and too cold to get the Tube, I looked at my watch and calculated I still had enough time to meet Luke and his friends for a drink. I should, of course, have done that in the first place, but it was no good: the routine of going to the office and eating lunch nearby was ingrained into my daily ritual.

Maybe it was sloth, looking for the easiest option, instead of doing what I really wanted to do. I think I reasoned I'd be seeing him later anyway. Besides, Luke was with his friends. They didn't want me there.

On reflection, they seemed lame excuses. I felt as if I'd been hypnotised by my own habits.

Outside the pub, the taxi driver asked for his fare.

'No, please wait,' I ordered.

He let out a groan. At times it can be very difficult to wait. Waiting is, perhaps, the hardest thing any human being ever has to do, with listening coming a close second. I avoided saying this to the driver, though.

Anyway, I thought, *Your meter is ticking, Mr Cabby.*

As I pushed open the door, I was greeted by dazzle and glare. Packed with locals, the pub brayed, neighed, gabbled, bleated, mewled, moaned and groaned. It was like a famous hangout for overacting thespians.

Where was Luke in all of this?

I stood under a flight of stairs that led to the small upstairs theatre. I tiptoed, clutching a balustrade so that I could stay upright as the room tilted, full of laughter. I couldn't see Luke and decided to get out.

It was then I realised I couldn't move. I tried putting one foot in front of the other, but the crush made it impossible. I couldn't budge.

'Excuse me, make way.'

The more I pushed forward, the more I was pushed back.

I began to feel desperate, but suddenly I sprang forward. I literally stumbled onto the street but, unlike others, it wasn't a movement caused by alcohol.

'Over here! Over here! Over here!' repeated the taxi driver, like a parrot.

'Take me home,' I said, closing my eyes. 'That was a nightmare.'

I took as deep a breath as I could.

'Where's home, sir?'

'The next turning after the square.'

The driver put the taxi into gear, opened the partition window wider and then spoke of something completely unrelated to our shared time together.

'You know guv, I remember an acquaintance of mine went as photographer on an expedition to climb some of the highest mountains in the world. He found that, not being a full-time mountaineer – and therefore not being used to thin air, thick snow, perpendicular rock and all that – the only way for him to survive was to scream an oath each time he took a step forward. That's how he dealt with the danger, if you understand me?'

The cab pulled up at my house. I took out the fare and gave him a generous tip. 'Thanks for that, guv. You know, if you hadn't asked me to wait, I doubt I'd have remembered that story about my friend. Have a happy Christmas.'

∴

Luke was highly embarrassed about something or other. I looked at him, he looked at me. We were each having as much difficulty as the other in keeping a straight face.

The charity dinner was reaching its conclusion and a game of bingo had been organised as the entertainment. Luke had been seated next to a fat lady wearing a bile green dress with faded gold brocade at the shoulders and cleavage. It was a tight fit all round, especially at the appropriately aristocratic bosom.

So who was complaining? Luke was, a little, because the lady had clearly taken a shine to him.

'Can we go?' he mouthed.

I grinned and mouthed back, 'What, now?'

'Yes!'

'No!'

'Play up! Play up! Play the game!' the bingo caller announced. 'Eyes down!'

Off we went, even those of us who were averse to numbers.

I noticed some bingophiles had more than one card on the go. In fact, several participants tackled the game with strange gusto, rolling up their sleeves. Luke joined in and mockingly took off his jacket. He signalled me to follow.

'Go on, Dad.'

Oh, how simple and beautiful life can be, sharing a joke with your child, no matter how trivial. I remember what I thought, at that moment, in that minute.

He'll charm the girls forever. He's got the smile of an angel and irresistible charm.

The first number to be called was, 'Two little ducks – twenty-two.'

Odd, isn't it, how we, or at least I, can remember such silly details while forgetting so much else? My birthday is 22nd July. What a coincidence!

'Lucky for some – number seven.'

As the numbers were called out, I was resistant to the whole process at the beginning. But then I found myself becoming more than interested: I was immersing myself in the game.

Help! I wanted to win!

I found myself with only one number left to get. Luke and I could share our silly story about my bingo triumph for years. I could even hear Luke telling his friends, 'Dad won the damn thing!'

One player leant over to another and, on hearing a number called out, said, 'Hey! You've got that one on your card!'

'Mind your own business,' came the reply. 'Play your own game.'

Almost there. Come on…

Come on!

Someone must yell soon, surely?

I was astonished by how long a game of bingo could take.

Home is wherever you are, you know. The answer is always at home, assuming you've learned to make your home where you are – oh, and also know how to feel at home when at home.

If you have God in your room, you have Heaven on earth....
God, as I do understand you.
Forgive me my trespasses ...

'All the sixes, clickety click – sixty-six!'

A voice shattered the silence and my internal conversation with God, with all the force of an alarm clock.

'BINGO!'

I recognised the voice. Was it my son? I turned.

Yes. It was Luke's.

He grinned the widest ever grin. 'BINGO!'

'You win some, you lose some,' the fat lady said, trying to console herself.

The organiser of the event called out for Luke Hammond and presented him with his prize. A small trophy, the size of an eggcup.

'Pose with your father,' he suggested.

Luke beckoned me over. 'Come on, Dad. I don't think we have one photograph of us together.'

My son was right. With all the many photographs I'd taken down the years, there were none of just the two of us.

Luke put his arm around my shoulder. We stared ahead into the lens.

FLASH! went the camera.

'I shoot only in black and white,' said the photographer, in a deep and aristocratic voice.

(We learned he was apparently a distant relative to the Queen).

'It gives a timeless quality,' he added, taking out an expensive-looking silver pen from his inside pocket and writing down my name and address. 'I'll send you a print as soon as it's developed. Just after Christmas, I imagine. It's a busy time …'

He made to pass his pen to me.

'No, I think that's yours,' I said, handing it back.

He let out a loud chuckle. 'I always seem to be doing that. Must be my age. I'm fifty, would you believe?'

Before he left to take more photographs, he gave me his business card, having first added his personal number and signature with a near-illegible flourish. It was the type of signature produced by those in positions of authority who presume recognition of their identity precedes them without any need to write it down, or should that be without anyone having to read?

∴

As the two of us stepped out onto the street from the party, it was beginning to rain and each drop of water felt like a table tennis ball hit by an opponent who started with gentle rallies but became more heated. Soon there were a thousand participants not using balls and bats at all, but scalpels and machetes and machine guns and cats and babies.

And everyone was winning and everyone losing.

Existence itself had come to the decision that, if it was going to end, it was going to end with a bang.

'Let the rains bedraggle me out of recognition!' Luke cried out, getting drenched. 'Long live this storm!'

Quite suddenly, without warning, he grabbed my arms and gave me a tight hug under the pouring rain.

Hold me, my son!

The world paused and I looked deep into his eyes. I should, at that moment, have said 'I love you' – but instead, I muttered something irrelevant, like, 'Did you know that in wartime, a storm meant there'd be no bombing that night?'

It's funny how we waste words and dismiss the opportunity to say things we really want to say.

I looked up at a sky brightened from below by street lamps. The drink was having its effect on me, with a phalanx of jack-booted clouds goose-stepping towards us, splinters of red shrieking as they were stampeded off into the middle of the city.

What was that about? I thought to myself.

I shook my head to regain my senses.

'Dad, let's go to your club to celebrate my victory and toast our Christmas!'

'Remind me, are you old enough?'

Luke smiled and said, 'Old enough to get drunk with my father!'

We both laughed then. Not like father and son. More like best friends.

∴

The club was usually a rather dour place smelling like a musty old room, never used. Tonight, though, it was a scene of unexpected, almost riotous, joviality. There was scope for gin and flirtation. The barstools offered confidence and chat.

'The usual?' the barman asked, with the tone of an excited schoolboy on the last night of term.

'Fire away,' said I, displaying the cleft in the middle of my chin.

'Fire!' shouted the barman, pouring a single malt bang into the middle of the glass.

'And the same for my son.'

'Is he old enough?'

The barman studied Luke's crestfallen reaction.

'I'm sorry, Master Hammond. I was only kidding!'

'I wouldn't worry,' I said to the barman, 'I played the same joke on him, only a few minutes ago.'

It was debatable whether he should joke like that, given his multiple capacities as barman, controller of a discrete door at the back of the bar and confidant privy to the details of members' lives. But, he was certainly not a bad man. I could trust him to help any friend in need. He passed over the drinks and eyed me with a cocktail of bonhomie and bluster, with a dash of tiredness.

We looked around to decide where we were going to sit. We headed for the furthest alcove. Alcoves were usually occupied by the solitary and the seducers. The solitary would slink away with their resentments, while the seducers conjured casuistry. But not that night. The room was bursting with happiness – a sense of bliss I've not encountered since.

How wonderful. For me, for Luke, for the two of us.

'Time for a quickie?' shouted a man who looked remarkably like Sherlock Holmes, his voice fired over people's heads towards a beautiful woman dressed as a jet-set gypsy. 'Come on! It is Christmas after all!'

The woman had a spotted crimson scarf, held in place by maroon braiding over her head, with two enormous earrings dangling in her soup. She waved a 'no thank you' at the man.

Luke found this very funny. He roared with laughter.

'Dad, don't look now,' he began, 'but there's a gorilla standing right behind you.'

Sure enough, there was. On closer inspection, I could make out a parade of members and friends in fancy dress.

'And just behind you, Luke,' I replied, 'there's someone dressed as a sea snake.'

Luke turned. 'It's a mermaid, Dad!'

'Oh. Are you sure?'

'Sorry to bother you,' interrupted a gentleman dressed as Charlie Chaplin. 'Do you mind if I have a word with your son?'

'Go ahead.'

'Excuse me, young man, would you mind judging our fancy dress competition? Our so-called celebrity has failed to show up and we're in a bit of a pickle. Can you step in? It would be a privilege to have someone from the younger generation to act as judge and present the prizes.'

How could he refuse?

'There will be four prizes, announced in reverse order.'

Luke squeezed my hand and joined Charlie Chaplin on the plinth. He spent a moment judging and then nodded, as if to say he'd made his mind up. There was a drumroll from the live band, which had been set up in the corner like an afterthought.

It felt like anyone dressed inappropriately was going to be guillotined.

I fiddled with my bow tie to reassure myself.

Luke started to speak into the microphone but no sooner had he said, 'What an honour …' than it began to squeal like a pig on its way to the slaughterhouse.

Charlie Chaplin took it from Luke's hand and blew down it as if he knew a secret magic trick.

'That's better,' he said, handing it back.

The microphone was now miraculously tuned.

In fourth place was the Gorilla. Luke handed him an envelope and said, 'very well done' like a pro who'd done it many times before. The gorilla accepted his prize (two free drinks from the bar) with a bow that expanded, like an accelerated film of a flower opening, into a monster curtsey. He then grabbed the microphone from Luke.

'I am very proud,' the man said. 'Better than fifth, eh? And mucho better than naught!'

As he walked back to his table, he received what could be euphemistically called moderate applause. He was given hearty handshakes from a flying fish, two queens and a quean.

Some people, I noticed, didn't applaud at all. Maybe they were the sort of people that just didn't applaud anyone or anything?

The third prize (three free drinks) went to the Mermaid (or flying fish, or whatever it was). She shimmered through the crowd, picked up her prize, was greeted by a rainfall of applause and quickly glittered back the way she'd come, a smile on her seraphic, if not fishy, face.

Second was James Bond.

Where is he?

My God, they were looking at me, as was my son! I was in a competition I didn't even know I'd entered.

I smiled graciously – or should I say embarrassingly – and, as I picked up my envelope prize (four free drinks), I detected a few 'Who's that?' and 'Fix!' catcalls, accompanied by a smattering of applause.

'You'll be accused of nepotism,' I whispered into Luke's ear.

Then there was a gasp, followed by a hush.

And the winner is…

Another drum roll dragging out the climax…

The winner is …

Of course it was …

The jet-set gypsy!

The club broke into tumultuous clapping, the sort you hear on TV quiz shows, when you know an applause board has been held up in front of the audience. The woman picked up her envelope (ten free drinks) and gave Luke a big kiss on his cheek. He blushed. Turning, the woman moved forward and gave a deep curtsey, mouthing thanks that were spoiled by the Gorilla choosing that moment to collapse onto a table. The heat inside his heavy, hairy costume must have been too much.

Luke grabbed hold of his head and wrenched it off.

'I was suffocating!' growled the Gorilla. 'Young man, you saved my life! The heat was unbearable!'

'Breathe deeply, Gorilla. Relax!' I heard Luke counsel.

Charlie Chaplin interrupted by offering the judge a drink on the house. The Gorilla growled and offered him a bottle of champagne. Added to my second-place prize, we could end up drinking until the early hours for no extra cost.

Luke marched over. 'What are you having, Dad?'

'A glass of wine.'

Luke's face fell. 'Come on, Dad, we only live once!'

He was right.

'Hey,' I called after him, changing my mind. 'Get me something different. Something strong and warming.'

'That's more like it,' he said, wringing his hands like the owner of a curry house when a customer asks for something really hot, but the owner knows it will blow their taste buds away.

I looked at Luke. His elbow was resting on the bar, his chin on his hand as if he were thinking. The barman dragged a bottle out from behind, wiped off the dust, and carefully poured out some of its contents. After he'd poured two glasses, I overheard him say, 'There you are. This should make you or break you.'

I thought of Kate. How proud she would have been of our son. What a gorgeous boy he'd turned out to be. I remembered when Kate was diagnosed with cancer. I'd been worried about Luke: how exposed he was about to be, to the brutality of life. We decided to be honest and tell him that his mother was going in for treatment. We sat him down and told him Mummy wasn't well and would have to take strong medicine.

'It's going to make my hair fall out,' Kate said, running her long fingers through her son's hair.

Silence followed silence and my heart screamed for a distraction. This wasn't right. It was a mistake to even discuss it. We should have waited instead, for his questions. But then Luke put his hands around his mother's waist and rested his cheek on her chest.

'Don't worry, Mummy,' he said. 'Hair grows back much better after the medicine. Only the other day, I overheard you wishing you had thicker hair.'

The memory made me melancholic. I sat silent and forlorn, like a bomber pilot after a raid from which more than half his comrades failed to return.

Sherlock Holmes was making a rather loud burping noise in the background that thankfully disturbed me. He caught my glare. I quickly turned away. I didn't want to set off down the road of silent interrogation.

∴

'Here we go!' Luke said. 'I've been advised you need to drink it in one.'

'Are you sure?'

'Absolutely!'

The muscles on his face tightened. I drank it in one.

Shoot! Wham! Bang!

After three seconds, steam gushed out of my ears, my nose spun like a top, my taste buds were blown away. The back of my head flew off but by then the alcohol had deadened my mouth and was threatening to announce itself to my brain, then to indelibly imprint itself upon my liver.

Luke gulped his down without any pain, not even a grimace.

'Another?' he asked.

'I think you'd better get me ... The bottle,' I gasped.

'Are you sure? That could be rather dangerous.'

'I can take it!' I said, trying to prove myself to my son through drink. 'Just watch me. You wait here.'

So I got up and negotiated my way towards the bar.

'A bottle of whatever you just poured for me and my son.'

The barman looked at me with an expression that suggested there was little doubt in his mind as to where I was heading.

'I'll bring the bottle over, sir. It will be safer that way.'

'No, I can do it.'

But the barman insisted on carrying the bottle himself.

'Not eating tonight, Mr Hammond?' he asked, setting the bottle and two glasses down on our table.

'We already have,' said Luke.

'That's good. Best not to have this on an empty stomach.'

Luke poured and kept the bottle on his side of the table. 'I'll take care of this,' he said.

It hadn't taken long for Luke to take charge. In many parts of our lives, as he grew older, he took control. I loved him for it. I never wanted to appear weak, though. I always wanted to demonstrate to him that, yes, I had the necessary strength with which to confront all adverse situations and adversaries, cope with all calamities.

I sat. Chin up. Back straight. Looked at the glass and – ugh! Drank it in one! A drink I had never seen or tasted before, or since that night. I squinted at the bottle but couldn't begin to decipher the hieroglyphics on the label. It was definitely strong stuff. The floor tilted further and further and further away, like a huge and slow-rocking chair at a funfair.

'Dad, you dropped these.'

Luke handed me some banknotes that had fallen to the floor.

God, how drunk was I? I coughed one of those long, phlegmy spasms one tends to hear coming from the room next door in thin-walled, cheap hotels. From my son's expression, I was reminded that he hadn't seen his father in this state before.

Luke took a deep breath.

'I feel as if I'm at the top of a white-knuckle ride,' he said. 'As if I'm hanging from a roller coaster that's broken down in mid-air. I'm holding on for my life!'

'It's funny, I think I'm at the funfair, too.'

Luke picked up the bottle by its neck and somehow it slipped from his hand, crashing to the floor.

We looked at each and burst into laughter.

And we laughed and laughed.

The barman came over promptly and didn't make as much fuss as I'd expected. He swept the mess up and away, as if he knew the mishap was bound to mis-happen. He returned to the bar and came back, placing another bottle down in front of us, not quite the same but a close relative.

The drink paralysed us. We didn't have the strength to send it away. We stared at each other until Luke let out a loud hiccup.

'Drink backwards out of your glass,' I advised him.

'Not with that I won't,' Luke said, nodding at the bottle.

'Well, what you need is a good fright,' I said, lurching forward at him. But it did nothing. He hiccupped again.

'Try holding your breath as if you're underwater.'

He did, for a moment. But then we both started to laugh

again. We were enjoying ourselves with something we could accept we were powerless over.

Alcohol. Father. Son. People. Places. Things.

'Did you know there are two thousand conversations like this one taking place on this earth right now?' Luke said.

'And there are some two thousand storms like the one outside, taking place right now around the globe,' I replied.

'And lightning strikes a hundred times a second.'

'And, for that matter, there are some two thousand squabbles.'

'I doubt it.'

'I hope not,' I said, and then remembered. 'You know, Luke … I saw an extraordinary effect in the sky this evening. It was as if we were in the middle of nature's abattoir.'

Luke must have misheard because he said something quite odd.

'Yes, and almost a quarter of a million people once died in a few days because those in charge believed artillery could destroy barbed wire.'

We went on until the early hours of the morning, the two of us intending to put the world to rights, until the barman called time and we caught a taxi. Luke was dropped home first. His final words of the night came as he slipped away to the other side of awareness.

'Who wants to be told anything, or saved from anything, right now?'

'Good night, Luke,' I told him. 'My darling son.'

The light of the moon followed him to his front door, key in hand, mumbling to himself. He turned to me before closing the door, with the most beautiful smile.

'Sleep well,' I mouthed.

' Sleep well, Daddy.'

∴

I woke with a start, wondering where I was. The silence of sleep had been shattered by the telephone ringing and by a pneumatic drill from the street, which shook the entire house.

I leaned over and picked up the phone.

'Dad,' a voice croaked.

'Are you feeling as rough as I am?'

'No, I feel good,' replied Luke.

'Really, how is that possible?'

Age, I thought.

'You won't forget to pick me up at three? I need to be at the airport by four.'

'Don't worry, everything is under control,' I said.

As I did, I looked at my bedroom, which was totally out of control.

'You mustn't let me drink, Luke,' I said. 'It isn't good for your old man.'

'But we had fun, didn't we? Don't forget I'm the bingo champion of something or other.'

'I won't forget. I plan to have that photograph of you, holding the cup, framed. I intend to give it pride of place in the house.'

Luke let out a laugh. 'You always wanted me to be a champion, didn't you?'

And he put down the receiver not waiting to hear my reply.

I'd decided before our night out not to go into work the day after. I was due some holiday, so I was taking two weeks off, including Christmas and New Year.

I was going to visit my sister in Cornwall the following morning. I planned to leave early to avoid the dull motorways and take the more interesting back roads that showed England at its best. I always enjoyed going down there. Nothing was ever too much trouble for my sister.

The year before, when I was down there with Luke, she'd looked after me without a single complaint, when I badly twisted my ankle and was confined to bed for a week. It had happened in the middle of the night, when I'd needed another blanket. At first, it wasn't cold enough for discomfort to direct me out of bed and triumph over sloth. But soon the temperature dropped even lower, so I climbed out of bed.

When something hurts enough, we do something about it.

I walked out of my room and across the landing. As expected, I found an extra blanket at the bottom of the airing cupboard. I shook it, in order to get rid of any creepy-crawlies I imagined might've sneaked in.

(Another hangover, not from drink but from a year I spent in South America, full of scorpions, spiders, snakes and 'what the hell is that?')

Somehow I shook the blanket so hard, it got trapped under my foot and I slipped, like an ice skater, flat on my arse. In the process I badly twisted my ankle and woke up the entire house. For the rest of our stay, I was confined to bed.

It was not the best Christmas.

By rushing to work every morning, I tended to miss the chaos

I left behind for poor Lidia, my loyal Portuguese maid. I'd never been able to tidy. I sometimes justified this character defect by repeating a quote that it showed, *I am living a full life, my energies being spent on more important matters.*

Still, I felt a little shamefaced when I heard the front door opening. I hastily pulled the sheets tight, shook a couple of cushions, congregated objects in the bathroom. But it was no help. The place looked as if a bull had crashed through it, or as if it had been pulled apart by thugs in search of jewellery.

Oh well. It was, in all honesty, nothing new.

Luke, who in his teens should have been at the peak of his own messiness, was always picking things up after me. When his fussing irritated, I would blurt out the old adage that boring people have tidy kitchens. As a student, my behaviour pattern was basically: expect a visitor, tidy the room, wait, give up hope, wait, wait, regain hope, wait, wait, wait, give up again until, by the time the visitor arrived, the place was a shambles from stuff having been thrown about, kicked at, torn up.

We can't forecast who or what is going to turn up or not turn up in our lives. We can't always arrange things to our complete satisfaction, either. However organised we might think we are, we can become unmanageable again at the click of one frustrated finger or with the swipe of an angry hand.

Lidia brought up my coffee.

'Good morning, sir. Did we sleep well?'

'I slept like hell, thank you. I'm a little fragile today,' I said. 'Just put the coffee on the dressing table.'

She threatened to open the curtains.

'Leave those!'

She looked put out. 'I see sir had a late night.'

'Late but fun. Luke and I had a Christmas drink together.'

I wasn't sure if she was listening. She'd picked up my dinner jacket, which had been hanging haphazardly, having been flung onto a chair in the early hours.

'I'll send this to the cleaners,' she said, and left the room.

I showered, dressed and slapped aftershave on my face as futile cover for the fact that I hadn't shaved. I looked in the mirror. What a sight. A hopeless case! The tossing and turning had aged me overnight. I'd had the most unsettling and inconsistent sleep, like a man under interrogation kept from sleeping properly by his torturers. I could have gone right back to bed at that moment. Was there anything in the world as disagreeable as being so tired you found it difficult to stay awake? But I had to get going. I had to pick the car up from the garage.

Knowing the track record of most garages, there would be a wait involved.

By the time I'd finished dressing and was ready, the time was well past eleven o'clock on that December morning. As I made my way downstairs, I stopped in my tracks.

Lidia was on bended knees, fingers linked together.

I coughed artificially as a warning.

'What are you doing?' I asked, knowing.

'I'm praying, sir.'

'Why, for Heaven's sake?'

'Because prayers work,' she said phlegmatically.

III

I read in *The Times* that a paperboy had been murdered after interrupting a serious robbery. He found himself in the hackneyed wrong place, at the wrong time. The burglars had grabbed him and, guessing he would be unable to keep his mouth shut, first threatened and then killed him by 'repeatedly holding his head underwater till the movements of his limbs were no longer part of his resistance'.

Without thinking, I scribbled down on a piece of paper *WRONG PLACE AT THE WRONG TIME* in block capitals and began to doodle jottings around each letter.

The telephone rang and I picked it up without looking.

'Yes, yes, yes,' the person on the other end of the line said, then sighed. 'Sorry. Wrong number.'

I put down the phone, again without looking, and turned to the paper's back page. I started on the crossword. *One across: waxed, so it can wane. Five letters.* I had no idea and immediately felt the frustration of having to wait another day until I got the answer. The telephone rang but again it was the wrong number. I walked over to the arranged breakfast table and poured cereal into a bowl.

Lidia walked in, holding up a shopping bag with Luke's sweater inside.

'Good, I was wondering where that was. Would you put it by the front door so I don't forget it?'

'For Luke?' asked Lidia.

'Yes ...'

The telephone started to ring again and, as Lidia walked over to answer it, I said, irritably, for the second time that morning,

'Leave it!'

Poor love. She must have thought I was turning into a monster.

I did think I heard her mumble, 'No more drink for you.'

I felt like a juggler that morning. I'd seen one in cabaret, in Berlin a few months before. He set some plates spinning on the top of thin poles, and then turned to face the audience in order to tell a story. When one or more of the plates began to wobble behind him, on the verge of crashing to the stage floor, he'd apologise to us and, as if he had eyes in the back of his head, would turn and set them spinning again. We ended up both listening to the story and watching the poles. Our attention tilted towards the former when the narrative was particularly exciting, but towards the latter when a plate was seemingly about to fall.

The noise from outside was starting to resemble the sound of a dentist's drill I imagined to be fast approaching my mouth.

I needed another coffee. I switched on the kettle and dropped two large spoonfuls of ground coffee in the fresh coffee press. I reached out for the milk bottle and somehow it crashed to the ground.

I felt like that juggler and let out a grunt.

'I'm out of here!'

Where had I left my car keys? Oh yes, at the garage. Wallet. Okay. I've got everything. Good!

'I'll see you tomorrow, Lidia.'

Just as I was turning the doorknob on the front door, she came rushing down the stairs. Without a word, she handed me Luke's airline ticket.

'What would I do without you?' I asked her.

I slipped the ticket into an inside pocket of my overcoat and made a hasty exit onto the noisy street.

∴

I grew fidgety waiting for my car. It was my first visit to this particular garage. My old, long-time mechanic had sold up and moved out of London. So, that was why I was here, and going to a new garage is always challenging – a bit like visiting a barber for the first time.

'Why's it taking so long? It's just a service and MOT.'

'Just an MOT?' laughed Barry the mechanic.

'I need to pick my son up by three and get him to the airport by four for a six o'clock flight.'

He glanced at his watch and said, 'You've plenty of time.'

An advertising sign, flashed above the garage like a truism.

IF LIFE WAS EASY EVERYBODY WOULD BE DOING IT!
IF LIFE WAS EASY EVERYBODY WOULD BE DOING IT!!
IF LIFE WAS EASY EVERYBODY WOULD BE DOING IT!!!

Just relax, I thought. *There's nothing I can do. If the worst comes to the worst, we can hail a cab and probably get there quicker than if I take my car.*

One hour and four coffees later, I was shown to my vehicle.

'As good as new,' Barry said.

I accepted his brief wet-fish handshake, incongruous with his brawny, tattooed forearm. I disliked him and guessed he disliked me. Such an immediate reaction still unsettles me. A large part of my upbringing was to 'love thy neighbour' and I'd tried to instil the same value into Luke. I had, though, recently fallen from grace – my bruised innocence coming up with the compromise that, in cases of instinctive dislike, I could move to the other side of a room and, if contact was inevitable, get it over with as quickly as possible.

These thoughts were going through my mind as I drove to Luke's flat.

∴

I sounded the car's horn. I switched on the radio and a commercial station was discussing the day's politics. My eyes were slowly focusing on the blue door to Luke's building, when my peace was disturbed by a knock on the window. It was Luke, ready, wearing a blue overcoat with a spotted scarf, tied around his neck in the way a pirate would have done it.

'Dad, open the back?'

I detected a slight smile on his opaque face. After all, he had something to celebrate: he was heading to New York City for Christmas.

'Oh, sorry.'

I clambered out of the car to give him some help. He had two bags, a brown suede and a small blue one, which I understood to be carrying presents for his girlfriend.

There was a silence as we drove off, as if we were allowing angels to pass overhead. When we reached the Hammersmith flyover, I looked up at a billboard of a breakfast cereal. A smiling tanned face stared down at us. It was as if his eyes (albeit poster eyes) were watching us. I half-expected the mouth to suddenly open and say something.

'He looks like you,' I said out loud.

Luke's hands grabbed for a piece of fluff as it fell.

Lucky if you catch it, so the superstition goes.

His fingers touched, even momentarily interlocking, but none could get hold of it. The fluff dropped to his shoes.

'Everything all right?' I asked.

My question interrupted Luke's daydream.

'Sorry, Dad, I am a little distracted. I'm not sure what's got into me.'

'Hangover?'

'Life's a hangover,' he said, unsure.

We started talking, slowly at first, quite unlike how we usually were together. As we approached the Hammersmith flyover, a line of traffic had already begun to form because of two cones blocking one lane. None of the drivers were quite sure how the line should form. It reminded me of a line when a bus has gone a few yards past the stop and people are trying to be honest about who was originally in front of whom.

'No, you go first.'

'No, please, after you.'

I picked up a cassette and put it in the player. Luke gestured to turn the volume up, higher and higher. So much for the hangover theory. He started to conduct with his index fingers, like a conductor who can direct a whole symphony without a score, not because he wants to show off but because he genuinely knows every single note of every single instrument and doesn't want to be influenced by the print.

I couldn't resist smiling at his pure joy, listening to something he loved.

It was *Eleanor Rigby*.

I don't know how many people I've asked, but can it be wrong to trust intuition? One should at least investigate it, surely? As the song finished its last bar (or did it simply fade?), I remember having a feeling of unease, much like a dog when an earthquake is looming. Maybe it's dangerous to rely on such instincts? I certainly didn't even mention it, for it was fleeting, like so many of our thoughts.

I switched off the cassette player. I sensed something wasn't quite right.

Scenes from that journey have flickered over the years. I'm no longer sure of anything.

'Dad?'

'Yes?'

'Do you promise me that in the New Year, you'll leave the City and open that bookshop you've always talked about?'

I laughed. 'Where did that come from?'

'I'm not sure.'

'Is that what's been on your mind?' I asked.

'Yes, among other things.'

What did he mean by other things?

A jet crossed the sky on its way to Heathrow. Maybe it was Luke's, landing to fill up with fuel before heading to New York.

Now, looking back, I'm sure it was. The very one.

I swivelled my head a fraction and glimpsed the plane's undercarriage and its lights, reflecting against a darkening sky that produced ever-changing shapes, angles and colours, like the continual stir of the ocean.

'I suppose I don't have enough courage,' I said.

'I think you do!'

It sounded like a demand.

'Typical,' I said, changing the subject.

As if from nowhere, another traffic jam had begun to form.

'It's okay, we have plenty of time,' Luke said.

But the cars were hardly moving. The line would jolt forward and then suddenly stop, like a chopped-up worm slowly coming back together. Soon, 'plenty of time' turned into voiced concerns of 'if I miss this flight, when is the next?'

It wasn't long before it became clear why the traffic had slowed: there had been an accident on the inside lane. Flashing lights were visible on an ambulance as it sped by.

Luke switched the car radio back on and we immediately got the traffic news:

'If you are heading to the airport this evening, avoid the M4 as there has been an accident and a long queue is forming.'

'Damn!' I said, punching the steering wheel.

'Hey calm down, it'll clear soon,' Luke said with certainty in his voice. And he was right, because the accident had happened just half a mile from where we'd slowed; soon, the sluggish trickle of cars began to filter through. Still, it was tight whether he'd make the flight, a situation not helped by drivers stretching over to get a better view and be witnesses to a mangled body.

I hooted the car in front. 'Move it!'

Luke tapped me on the hand.

'I'm just trying to get you there, that's all.'

I squeezed his fingers, twice.

As soon as we passed the accident, the road ahead was clear. It was as if an empty stretch had been ordained. It wasn't long before we reached the outskirts of the airport, and the Heathrow tunnel seemed to suck us in. Once inside, the car gently lost touch with the world outside. I heard the muted sound of overhead jets and the rumble of the car engine bouncing off the curved walls. The hum from the main road became fainter and fainter as we were pulled further down the tunnel, until suddenly we were in the centre of the airport.

'Listen, I'll park, you go check in. You'd better hurry!'

I looked at my watch for the hundredth time in the last five minutes, and got out to help with the bags while Luke found a trolley.

A traffic warden marched up, his face a discord of fury, tiredness and resignation.

'You can't park here,' he said.

'What?'

Luke gave me quite a shock by sharply grabbing my elbow.

'Leave him, Dad.'

'Haven't you got anything more important to do?' I asked the warden.

He put his fingers in his ears and shook his head.

I was about to say something else when Luke said, 'My tickets!'

'Shit!' I frisked my pockets. 'Shit, I know they're here somewhere.'

And then, like conjuring a rabbit, I pulled a folded envelope from my inside coat pocket.

'Here they are.'

'Have you checked if it's the right date?' Luke asked.

I made the decision to lie. 'What do you mean? Of course I have.'

It felt for an instant like I was claiming to have watched a movie I hadn't seen. The big difference this time was that I was going to be found out immediately.

Luke opened up the envelope and studied the tickets earnestly, like a judge about to announce the winner of Miss Universe.

A sinking feeling came over me. His mouth was shaped as if it had tasted sea salt. I closed my eyes for a moment and, when I opened them again, Luke was smiling.

'Just kidding!' he said. 'I'll see you inside.'

I must stop lying, I thought. *It isn't worth it!*

It's usually wiser to own up to ignorance than to feign with a convoluted lie. There isn't much that's more tedious than listening to someone talking about a movie they haven't seen.

∴

Insanity ruled Terminal 3. There was pandemonium. Christmas pandemonium. Was it excitement for their Christmas break, or fear that they were going to miss their flights? I manoeuvred through the kerfuffle and by the time I'd reached the Pan Am desk, Luke had just finished checking in his bags.

'You have a very charming son. I've found him a good seat,' the Pan Am attendant said.

'He's not bad, is he?' I squeezed his cheek with pride.

'Dad, please!'

It's said that if we hang around with certain people, a quality they possess but we don't have will somehow brush off on us, like pollen carried on a bee. In Luke's case, the quality was obvious: a self-possessed confidence, the sort that nobody and nothing could strip away. He was a light to those he encountered.

'You'd better hurry. They'll be closing the flight very soon,' the attendant said.

Luke glanced down at his watch – a Boucheron watch I'd given him for his birthday. We chased over to the passport desk. There was no line.

He turned and took me by the arms. 'Happy Christmas, Dad. I love you.'

'Goodbye, my boy. Have a wonderful time. Call me on Christmas Day.'

My son kissed me on the cheek; my left cheek, just below my left eye.

'Damn!' I clicked my fingers. 'I forgot the sweater I bought you. You know how cold it can get out there.'

'Don't worry. You can give it to me when I get back. It will still be just as cold here.'

He gave me a beautiful wide smile as the loudspeaker sounded his flight:

'PAN AM 103 TO NEW YORK. FINAL CALL.'

He handed his passport across the desk. The officer straightened his jacket and checked the passport briefly before handing it back.

'Happy Christmas!' I called out.

I wasn't the only one saying his goodbyes. Quite a crowd had gathered with long looks and messages shouted between cupped hands.

'They're emigrating to Australia,' the man next to me said, pointing at a rather dumpy couple with four young children approaching passport control.

'That's nice,' I replied.

At which point, he dropped his bag and some papers fell out, scattering around our feet.

'God!' the stranger said, leaning down to pick them up.

'Let me help,' I said. Bending down, I picked up a couple of the sheets. He piled them into his bag, placed it under his arm and proffered his lank fingers.

'Cheers,' he said, and sighed.

When I looked up, Luke had disappeared from view. It was odd, because although the noise surrounding me had grown even louder, I felt utterly alone.

The future at that moment seemed so far away.

∴

The journey home from the airport was frustrating. There was more traffic coming into London than going out. The car in front was belching black smut from its exhaust and a neighbouring coach had children staring and sticking out their tongues.

When I reached the Brompton Road, each traffic light flashed red as I was approaching. I was in no hurry – I'd made no plans for the evening – but it still irritated and accentuated my overall gloom. It wasn't helped when I saw someone on the lookout for a vehicle to approach before they pressed the button on the crossing.

As I unlocked my front door, I began to feel dizzy. I glanced down and was immediately drawn to the bag carrying Luke's sweater. The bag seemed to be swaying and I leaned against the wall for support. It was an odd sensation, not unlike being in a rail station when the train you're sitting in seems to leave but it's an adjacent train pulling away in the other direction, while yours remains standing.

My watch said it was 7.03PM. I looked up at the sky, to see if I might spot Luke's plane. Ridiculous, really; it would have been well on its way by then.

It seemed like the darkest of nights, under heavy cloud. Everything was quite still, an utter stillness never repeated again in my life.

I thought, *Lucky boy, to be flying across the Atlantic to meet your true love.*

I felt so happy for him.

I managed to regain some balance by the time I reached the kitchen. Lidia had left a note.

Dinner in oven – heat for 30 minutes – hope Luke got off okay.

I poured myself a glass of water. I didn't want to be sick, not with Christmas just a few days away, but no sooner had I drunk a few sips than I found myself running to the bathroom.

I retched. I retched. I retched again.

I looked into the mirror above the basin. What a sight! Such a pale prospect, my eyes squinting. I took a deep breath and put my head under the running water. Oh God, please don't let me be ill, not over Christmas...

And then, quite miraculously, I did feel a bit better.

Prayers work. Yes! So why don't I pray more often?

'Pray until something happens!'

Is it because I'm human and usually pray for the wrong things?

We pray for the way we want things to turn out, rather than for the ability to accept them, however they turn out. That's what I was thinking at that moment, at that very moment ...

Within a few minutes of washing my face, I decided to take a walk round the block to breathe slowly in the night air. Yes! How quickly things can change. Again. And again. Yet, as I was looking for my scarf, my search was diverted by a disconcerting noise coming from the drawing room.

That was odd. I couldn't find anything out of place. Maybe it was the rushing sound of the pipes below the radiator?

When I returned from my stroll, I switched on the television and turned up the volume. I bent down to turn the dial to BBC2, when a card with 'Newsflash' shone onto the screen and I heard a deep voice saying, 'before our next programme, we are going over to the newsroom and Nicholas Witchell.'

The eyes of a redheaded newsreader were suddenly on a level with mine.

His mouth moved, saying these words,

'GOOD EVENING. THERE'S BEEN A MAJOR AIR CRASH TONIGHT NEAR THE SCOTTISH BORDER. A PAN AMERICAN JUMBO JET CARRYING MORE THAN 250 PEOPLE HAS CRASHED NEAR THE TOWN OF LOCKERBIE IN DUMFRIES. THE FLIGHT NUMBER 103 WAS EN ROUTE FROM LONDON HEATHROW TO JOHN F. KENNEDY AIRPORT, NEW YORK. EYE WITNESSES IN LOCKERBIE SAY THE AIRCRAFT CRASHED NEAR A PETROL STATION. THERE WAS A HUGE BALL OF FIRE. LOCAL HOSPITALS HAVE BEEN TOLD TO PREPARE FOR MANY CASUALTIES. WE WILL HAVE MORE …'

A hint of a tingle changes into a shudder that shoots down me like a tremor along a fault line, when I realise that the words are being spoken to parents, brothers, sisters, friends of those on board …

To me.

Pan Am 103.

Pan Am?

103?

It's Luke's flight number!

I stood bolt upright, with the knowledge that my son was in trouble, not far away – not waving, but imploring, not shouting for joy ... but screaming in fear ...

'Luke! My son! My baby!'

My voice strangled the night.

It was the shriek of a pitiable creature being torn apart.

∴

I turned off the television. No more words were needed. The sooner I got there, the better.

He said casualties.

Hospitals. *Casualties.*

First, a roadmap.

I saw one only the other day, I thought. It was on my desk in the study.

I found it immediately, as if it were waiting for me.

I searched for Lockerbie.

'Small town, not far from the English border in the southwest of Scotland. Yes, he said Dumfries ... That is where he is ... M1, M6, A74. A straightforward drive ... Five, perhaps six hours? God! Luke is in Scotland. It will be cold, damn cold up there. The sooner I get there, the better.'

I put a sweater on and looked for my coat.

'I have to be ready. Now, where is Luke's sweater? Oh yes, by the front door. Good thing I forgot to give it to him. He'll need it now. I must get to Scotland. We must all live. My son must live.'

I looked at my watch. It was now 8.12PM.

I was in my car, map open at my side. I was heading for the M1.

I drove by Regent's Park. Everything looked so normal, so still, so calm …

Calm. Calm after the blaze of war or calm, calm, calm before more war, a worse war? Motionless, except for the crows' nests of the trees, which gave the slightest sway.

The oaks, beeches, silver birch! What trees! What beautiful words! Oh, it's been so long … Why have I not been more appreciative of trees? Forgive me, trees! Please! When I pick up Luke, I'll love you more than ever before! Concentrate. Hold the fucking wheel with both hands.

'Hurry up!' I shouted, putting my foot down even harder on the accelerator.

∴

A quote comes to mind.

I prefer not to forget, for then I don't suffer the pain of remembering.

I do not know how to write this. Or where. Or when. I feel like taking this blank paper to another hour and to another place, another life, into space, into another universe and time … It's as if I've been hoisted from my life by a crane, then lowered onto a train supposedly en route to a favourite place but diverted to a wrong track and crashed into the buffers.

Oh, that any of us can be so vain as to think we have even begun to understand anything.

∴

It was after midnight, so a pedant might say it was already 22nd December, but I can never think of a new day starting until the first light arrives, assuming it ever does again.

I had to pinch myself to realise what was happening, what I'd heard.

'I have to stop dredging the depths of my mind, concentrate on this road. He's waiting for me. He's cold. Damn, I don't have a hot drink! I rushed. I should've brought the thermos, yes, the thermos in the kitchen, under the sink. Made some tea. Luke likes it with milk. PG Tips. I should have slowed down, taken my time. At least I remembered the sweater. It's here, sitting on my lap.'

I touched the smooth wool.

'Shit! The price tag is still on. I'll have to take it off before Luke sees it.'

It was a long drive and I set myself tasks. I switched on the radio. I was on the M6. It was deserted. The announcer on Radio 4 had said many were dead.

Who is alive? Who is dead?

Which passers-by get caught in the crossfire of others' creeds, ferry passengers by one fool's failure to shut a door, whole countries by drought, war and famine?

Enough! Enough. There were many injured in Scotland. I had to understand that.

The radio news was full of gloom. Listening but not comprehending, I thought, *Did they just say it was bound for Detroit? Maybe I was confused and it wasn't the New York flight, after all? Maybe another Pan Am flight left at the same time. It can happen.*

'Maybe Luke missed the flight. Oh dear God, what are they saying now? Stay positive. There's bound to be life. Life is everywhere. Hope leads to hope. Hope leads to stability, sanity, to reality.'

I sank deeper into my seat. I was determined to stop the discussion going on in my head. I needed to relax, not think. When I reached the exit from the A74, I saw the first sign I may be nearing my destination. The bleak panorama from the car window added grey weight to my feeling that nature was a cheat, happiness a con, time itself a trick. Cars on the side of the road had been burnt out. On the horizon, fire rockets seem to rise and fall from a hail cloud.

It began to look like a war zone.

'Keep driving,' I kept telling myself. 'Clear the skies. You're nearly there. Turn off the radio.' Repeating: 'They don't know what they are talking about. Some are still alive. My son is still alive.'

I came to a halt. I banged on the side window with my forehead. Harder and harder.

Come on!

My fingers began to stiffen. The car heaved forward. We were beginning to move again.

Hold onto the wheel. Hurry up.

On the outskirts of Lockerbie, I hesitated, pleading to God to give me strength. I looked up to the sky. Searching for the aircraft? But instead, I saw stars. At first I saw very few of them, but the longer I looked, the more and more and more they appeared. And I found myself asking what was beyond the furthest star; how could you define nothing, let alone picture it; whether it was true our own galaxy was but a part of a greater galaxy that was part of an even greater galaxy; and, the faint band of light crossing the night sky, the Milky Way, made up of millions of distant stars, seemed to be moving in straight lines …

There! Six, twelve, all the sixes … I hear the distant sound of bingo numbers! Ah dear God, bring my mad mind down to earth.

What was I doing? I had my son to find.

'Can I help you, sir?'

It was a uniformed official wearing one of those fluorescent coats and shining a torch at the car.

I rolled down my window. I took in a deep breath.

'Good evening or rather good morning, officer. I am here to collect my son. He was on the plane, the Pan Am flight to New York. Could you direct me to where he might be? He must be very cold but it's okay, I have this sweater for him.'

I showed it.

He looked at me compassionately. 'Where have you come from?' he asked.

'I just drove up from London.'

'Sir, park here and come with me,' he said.

I was cold. I was very cold. An ill wind swirled between my eyes and the hand that carried the blue sweater. I could hardly walk. My hands trembled.

Luke needs the sweater, now.

I turned away from the glare coming from the burning buildings and into the black of the night (all of a sudden, very black). For an instant, I closed my eyes and heard the incessant rustling of the trees; I imagined a cold, wet, dark forest was out there in the distance.

'For Christ's sake, what is this place? Where is my son?'

I was led into the town hall. Lights were shining and phones were ringing, thumping in my ears. A woman sitting behind a desk seemed as if she were waiting for me.

'Would you like to sit down?' she asked.

'I'd prefer to stand.'

She then said, in a tone of voice used by someone stating the very obvious,

'I'm afraid there were no survivors.'

I took a deeper look, through the eyes, beneath the mouth. I asked her to repeat what she had just said to me.

'I'm very sorry but no-one could possibly have survived.'

This time I listened more carefully, between the words, through the sense, under the official claptrap.

I squeezed the sweater, feeling the warmth between my ice-cold fingers.

'Forgive me. I don't think you understand. My son is out there and getting cold. I have this for him.'

I held up the sweater.

'He needs it to keep him warm. I think he was wearing a coat but he'll still need this, you see, I bought it for Christmas. I just forgot to give it to him. He told me not to worry, he said he would be back soon and …' I swallowed a deep breath. 'He is okay. I know he is. He's out there waiting for me.'

I'd repeated those words on my drive so many times, I'd started to believe them.

'Would you like to speak to this gentleman?' She got up and mumbled something under her breath to a police officer who looked as if he had just returned from the outside. His trousers were damp, his face grey and forlorn.

I closed my eyes again and patterns began to roll, of black and white fireworks, a dozen tiny carousels.

Was I asleep? Maybe this was my dream?

I've been dreaming I was dreaming. That's it! The sort of dream very near to waking, so it feels real.

And then I heard the policeman's voice.

'Excuse me, sir – perhaps you would like to join me next door? We could get something to eat or maybe something hot to drink.'

A pulse throbbed in his temple.

The suggestion unsettled me, from past experience. A quiet chat is rarely positive. I followed him as if walking from the wings of a stage and/or still in my dream. Food was being served in a makeshift canteen still being set up. I sat down. I dug my fingernails deep into my palms and felt some pain.

Maybe I was awake after all.

The police officer went off and brought back two mugs of strong tea. PG Tips with milk.

'Drink this, it should warm you.'

He spoke calmly, kindly and very slowly.

I suddenly heard what had been said moments before.

'I'm sorry, there are no survivors.'

My mouth dried. I grasped the metal chair. I grasped the steel. Like glue. Tongue frozen to ice. Electric shock stuck.

I heard a faint but intelligible sound, yes, like a wounded animal's death cry through thick snow.

'They're late. Too late. We're all too late. It's too late,' I mumbled, shaking him firmly by the arm and then I said, without thought, 'What is it that decides who must die and when, and how, and why?'

The hall had filled up. Countless hurried conversations, none of which I could hear distinctly, except for one man, with a face so thin it was halfway to becoming a skull. He was sitting at the next table, talking too loudly.

'I saw the sky explode,' he said. 'As I looked up, my life flashed by, down a long, white tube. And just when there was a lull, parts of the plane surged towards us like a broken puzzle. It exploded. We didn't stand a fucking chance.'

Another. A local-sounding woman in her fifties with a soft, kind face.

'The cockpit is nearly intact,' she said. 'It's just three miles outside the town. The golf course is littered with bodies. Those poor, poor souls – and think of their families …'

Enough!

I got up and left the town hall. As I walked onto the path, I slipped and fell to the wet ground. A stranger offered his hand.

'I'm okay!' I shouted. 'I must find him. I have to find him. You see, I have this sweater.'

My feet froze to the stone and my eyes iced over as I saw figures turn, walk away, away from me, fading, fading, fading, fading into the night ...

Tears wanted to come to my eyes but at first they would not surface.

With throats unslaked, with black lips baked, we could not laugh or wail.

Yes, just like when I travelled down to tell Luke his mother had died. I unsteadily began to walk in the darkness, towards the open fields – but then I slipped, again, this time face down, my hands stung by flagstones, my lungs breathing in the dirt.

'Let the dirt soil my lungs.'

I tried to stand, but my legs simply gave up. I collapsed to my knees and raised the palms of my hands together and started to wail uncontrollably.

'What on Earth, what in Heaven am I doing?'

Since then I have cried a thousand tears, a million tears, a billion tears.

There would never be a day again that would pass without me weeping.

∴

When I was leaving Lockerbie, I vowed never to return, because death is truly locationless. The locationless is everywhere, and nowhere.

I decided, also, that I would never want to see his body.

I knew they'd find it. I just knew.

But no, I would remember him from our last night, and from the entirely precious, God-given days before.

That way I would never lose him. Never, never, never lose him.

∴

Driving back to London, the roads seemed empty. I limped home as unfeelingly as a drone. The early morning trains sidled past, carrying fallen faces; there was an anti-climax in the angle of arms resting on train window ledges.

I imagined the world sharing the same grief. I daydreamed, lost in thoughts triggered by the fading moon's shadow.

Most nights she is female, pale and bewitching. That night, she was fat with child. She spread a great tablecloth across the countryside, in preparation for the baptismal feast. She was beaming with pride. Yet, there was something disconcerting about her confidence, like that of a person in the public eye who makes an overt fuss over what he's going to name his forthcoming child, and is sent little blue socks or frilly pink frocks but, alas, he and his partner suffer a dreadful miscarriage.

This moon, too, will eventually lose her child and try to give birth again and again until the end of Time ...

∴

It took eight hours to drive home. I crept quietly into the house and straight into the clatter of a ringing phone. It seemed as if it had been ringing all night. I picked it up without thinking and heard the sound of stilted breaths down the other end of the line.

I heard my sister's voice asking gently if it was Luke's flight. If Luke was on Pan Am 103.

My silence gave her the answer. I said nothing.

'I'll see you soon,' she promised.

I slowly put down the phone and walked in to the kitchen. I was in desperate need of water. I was thirsty and tired. I opened the fridge. Everything looked the same as earlier and it was. All that had changed forever was me.

As I gulped down the water I saw Lidia's note still on the table.

… hope Luke got off okay …

I left the empty bottle of water on top of the piece of paper and walked upstairs. I paused at Luke's bedroom door. It was always his room. He may not have lived with me anymore, but whenever he visited he'd spend time in there. It was his space and I rarely invaded it.

The door was shut. I slowly opened it. I let out a grievous groan, as if a knife had been shafted into my stomach. I could still smell him and feel our last hug at the airport.

Oh, the boy, the teenager, the man.

I sat on the edge of his bed for a moment. *I miss you, Luke. I miss you.* I half-closed my eyes and saw Lockerbie and the outlying fields, through a mist of my own making. To hell with the imagination! I shook off my shoes. They were still soiled with Scotland's mud. I lay on Luke's bed and then slowly got under the covers. During those last remaining moments of awareness, I saw a terrified Luke running towards me through an overgrown meadow on a hot summer's night.

'Run, my boy! No, no, no, run faster. I'm here. I'm waiting for you.'

And as he got closer, his face began to relax, a sudden peace of death flowed through his body.

'Daddy! Daddy!' he cried.

The peace flowed as fast as Luke's footsteps had been on the dry earth.

He fell to the ground and lay quite still.

IV

Death is nothing at all ... I have only slipped away
into the next room.
... I am I, and you are you ... Whatever we were
to each other, that we are still ...

Following that night, I lost track of time. The clocks in my head were continually changing. I was living with the gangrenous guilt of having bought Luke his airline ticket, driving him to the airport and making it to the plane on time. I tried to persuade myself that the higher power wanted the beautiful to die young.

Ugh, the excruciating pain! The silent mourning. Why didn't we tell each other more often, more forcefully, how much we cared? Why didn't we hug each other more closely? I spoke to Luke constantly as if he were always close, near to my side. Things like, what do you think of this? What is the point of this?

Sometimes, I'd wake in the middle of the night and jot down more questions than answers: do you know when you're going to die, or not know when you're going to die? Do you know where you're going to die, or not know where you're going to die? Do you know how you'll die, or not? Die alone? Die in company? Die today? Die tomorrow?

Die right now or live forever.

Oh, and do you know what happens to you after you die, or not know what happens to you after you die?

Death consumed me. It was impossible to move my life on. I needed something, or someone, to force a change upon me.

∴

I was staring out of my bedroom window. I was looking out at the moon. It had become a sort of meditation during those days, like looking into a fire, watching the flames. There was almost a half-moon that night, one half being visible if you didn't look too carefully. I wondered if there was a hazy moral to that. Are we likely to see things more clearly if we don't look too closely? Are things more likely to happen if we don't try too hard?

Only as I looked and thought a little deeper did it strike me, this particular moon was surely waxing faster than normal. So, I'd been studying the moon for a few months and all of a sudden I was a lunar expert?

More like a lunatic! Surely the moon shouldn't be this full by now?

But then, I asked myself just how much or how little did I really know – about the moon or, for that matter, about anything else?

How, at my age, do I know so little? I know hardly anything, Luke.

I wasn't even sure whether, when a moon was full in this city, it was the same all over the Earth. Of course it was. Wasn't it?

But perhaps, as I've said before, I'd lost track of time. There were no rules when it came to time, as I'd learned, painfully.

I walked over to the whisky next to the television, poured the remaining contents of the bottle into a glass and gulped it as if I'd just emerged from a desert and it was water.

I opened the bedroom door and yelled down to Lidia to bring me up another bottle. She would, without question. She saw what it was doing to me but she also saw that, after several hours' worth of alcohol, it insulated me from the cold, sharp pain.

Like an alcoholic, I thought alcohol was helping. I would go out most nights to the local pub, sit alone, get drunk and, at closing time, walk the five streets and roads back home and then heave my guts out. From nausea. From hangover. From regret. From remorse. From grief.

Back to the bottle and the numbness.

Friends would call but I was distant and pleaded with them to be left alone.

'Let me mourn in peace.'

I had the only friend I needed. It may sound like a cliché but it was the bottle.

'Too much drink,' a stranger said in the bar one day.

I drunkenly replied, 'You should never accuse people of being drunk before you find out why they drink.'

'Lidia! Where are you?'

I returned to my window and concentrated on the stars. At first I saw very few of them, but the longer I looked, more and more of them appeared. And, with them, came habitual half-questions – pleasant ones, because I was aware I didn't know the answers to all of them, and probably never would. What was beyond the furthest star? How could you define nothing, let alone picture it?

'Everything must end somewhere,' grumbles a schoolchild, who can't get his or her head around the concept of recurring decimal places.

'It must all stop sometime, surely?' dreams the hobo, lying face-up on his park bench. 'All of it, including this sky – this day, night, life, world, universe ...'

'Excuse me, Mr Hammond, I'm sorry to disturb you but I have a friend,' Lidia said, as she replaced the empty bottle with a new one. 'She has a special gift and is very interesting. She talks to the dead.'

Interesting. A word I've always mistrusted.

I poured some whisky into my glass. At first I didn't touch it.

She talks to the dead? Isn't that what I've been doing? It's whether she can hear them that's important.

'Well, Mr Hammond? Would you like to see her?'

Lidia's question sobered me.

'Yes,' I replied, as a robot might. 'Please, arrange it.'

∴

The house had a tiny front door, probably because it was so very old. I knocked and knocked. I waited and waited. Maybe I'd got the wrong day? Or I was given the wrong time. It was still very early. As I stood out on the suburban street, countless voices were muttering in my head, like soft rain but growing heavier. I waited for the water to submerge me, for suffocation to begin. For my life to flash past me, down a long, white tube and into a dark tunnel.

Lidia had arranged my appointment a couple of days after mentioning it. I'd jumped to the top of the queue, I was told.

'She is in great demand,' Lidia boasted, and then muttered, 'I told her it was an emergency.'

And it was. Any possible means of communicating with my son was worth everything to try. In a way, it was my last hope.

The front door swung open.

'Sorry to keep you,' the clairvoyant said, strangely rubbing her hands in glee.

I gave a half-hearted echo, partly as a result of a deep, years-old sense of good manners.

'Follow me,' she said.

I entered not into a front room, but to a good-sized room at the back of the property. As I sank into an oversized chair, the walls converged as in a nightmare, until the space was like one of those claustrophobic, secret dungeons accessed only through a trapdoor. I used to read about those, in beautifully simple, action-packed stories as a child, on under-the-blanket torch-lit nights.

She asked if I would like some water, snapping me out of my dream state.

'Yes please. Is it very warm in here?'

'I'm not quite sure what you mean,' she said, clenching her teeth.

She passed me a glass and I knocked it back in one.

Ah, that was better. Or so I thought.

'Shuffle these and cut them into three piles.'

I was holding a pack of threadbare tarot cards, so worn I could hardly place one under another. After what can best be described as jumbling the cards, I handed them back to her. She dealt them individually into the shape of a Celtic cross.

I saw the card with Death marked on it straightaway.

'Interesting,' she said.

There goes that word again.

I let out a shiver and noticed a flash coming from the corner of the room. It seemed like the flame of a match, flick of a lighter or blade of a knife.

I thought, *Whatever it was, don't look.*

By the time I glanced over again, it had gone – presuming it had been there in the first place.

Her eyes flickered. 'Are you all right?'

'Oh, I was just hallucinating.'

'Mmm,' she said, and wrote something down in a notebook, appearing to take down my thoughts as dictation.

There was a pause.

'Now what?' I asked.

She looked into my eyes and I looked back into hers. Opposite me was this wizened, sour and anaemic face, marked with lines and wrinkles, even furrows. They were like scratches on a record that's been under-protected and over-played.

'You're angry. You're confused,' she said.

'I am?'

My ears were wide open but I was not listening.

'I've someone here in spirit. An old man …'

'My father perhaps?' I said it only to interrupt my head.

'He's here especially to see you …'

Why else would he be here, I thought.

And then I said, 'As a clairvoyant, you must resist self-doubt.'

'I beg your pardon?'

'Resist self-doubt. Even more, challenge the doubts of other people. Don't listen to anyone. Just keep going.'

She hesitated, looking at me for several seconds.

'Well, this is unexpected. It seems as if I am getting messages from you,' she said, letting out another laugh. 'It's true what you say. I've recently been accused of being a charlatan, by a malicious journalist from the local rag. I do have a gift, you know. I help many people every day. I have, in fact, helped nations discover oil.'

She closed her eyes as if she intended to take a doze and spoke theatrically about this old man, asking questions about him. Instead of just saying I had no idea what she was talking about and maybe she was the charlatan she'd been accused of being, I tried to guess the answers.

I needed to leave. I was beginning to feel a shortening of breath, my heart was starting to pound. I shouldn't have gone there. This was ridiculous.

'Was he a smoker?'

Maybe because of my seriously blank expression, she seemed to have had enough.

'I'll give you a free reading tomorrow if you'd like,' she said. 'I just don't seem to be on form today.'

'It's okay, really. I'm afraid I have to go. Excuse me,' I said, hurriedly shaking her hand.

Just as I was about to go, she said, 'But ... there is one last thing ...'

She paused. I gritted my impatience.

'I've a message from a young man. A handsome young man with a thick mane of brown hair and ...'

'Yes?'

'You should open your post. It's no good to anyone just leaving them there.'

I was startled by her statement. It was as unexpected as it was piercing.

'Go open each and every one of them. They will bring you comfort and maybe a few answers.'

I felt a tear fall from my eye.

'One other thing,' she continued. 'It sounds a little odd, but he says there is no need for the sweater. He is fine without it and it will come to you, who should have it.'

I buckled and pressed my hand against the wall for support. My heart had been stopped by her words, like she was an unwanted trespasser. Then it filled with warm relief, like the recognition that the trespasser was, in fact, a comforting friend.

'Thank you, thank you!' I exclaimed, giving her a hug.

She smiled and handed over a small card with italicised words on it. I tucked it away without looking, went out the door and down the street. Just before I reached the underground station, I took the card out and read the words aloud.

Each day in the past fades a little. Time heals, but does not cure.

∴

The post had indeed remained unopened. It had been left in a pile on the kitchen table, ever since that terrible night. Lidia was asked to leave them just on the edge, because that was where I'd opened post on the day Luke's airline ticket had arrived.

Strange how the mind works. I wanted everything to connect with my son in those days. I'd taken his favourite mug and left it out on the sideboard, looking as if it was ready and waiting to be filled and drunk from.

I sat at the table alone. I took a deep breath and started to open envelope after envelope. There were beautiful, intimate letters, some of them addressed directly to Luke.

Now that you have gone, dearest Luke, please understand I will never forget you ...
Goodbye my beautiful friend, I still feel you close, so close ...

I sat, without a break, reading each letter, every word that was, until I reached an envelope slightly larger than the others. It felt as if it had something inside, that somehow it was important. My name and address had been written by a shaky hand. I held the envelope up to the light and looked at it, with all the care of a stamp collector examining a rarity.

I went over to the sideboard to pour myself some whisky, but I hesitated and, probably for the first time in weeks, pushed the bottle away.

I looked again at the envelope and slowly opened it. Inside was a folded piece of paper, with two edges partially glued together. Using a kitchen knife, I slit the paper open and something fell out, a small card, the size of a playing card.

I looked at the sheet of paper first. It read, *Sorry for the wait – Thought you might like it in this new size I've been working on – Good to carry in a wallet! Best –*

The signature was illegible. I picked up the card. It was the photograph taken at the bingo party on the last night of my son's life, his right arm around my shoulders.

There was a pause and then I let out an icy scream.

Lidia came rushing down from upstairs. I was staring numbly ahead. I handed her the photograph.

I mumbled, 'Oh God, let me mourn in peace.'

'It is beautiful,' Lidia said and gasped slightly. She then said something innocuous that would change my life yet again. 'Why don't you go for a walk and get some fresh air? It's a surprisingly warm day.'

I thought a moment and said, 'You're right, it would do me good.'

As I was leaving the kitchen I spied the bottle of whiskey but again, I left it. I went in search of my overcoat instead.

∴

The streets were quiet. The sun took its hat off in the shape of a cloud. I moved at the pace of an old horse, or hearse, or old horse-drawn hearse. As I walked, my eyes went down to my feet.

Someone coughed into a microphone, out of nowhere. Was it for attention? Or was it a calling from God, because, as I looked up, I found I was being overshadowed by a church. The voice from the microphone sounded nervous and the words non-liturgical. No wonder. It was coming from inside the hotel next door, preparing for a wedding reception.

I gave a small chuckle and an invisible force pushed me inside the church.

I thought of my father as I walked in. He wasn't a religious man. In fact, the only religious conversation I ever had with him was pretty one-sided.

'Life can work if you don't believe in God but life won't work if you believe you yourself are God,' he'd said, and looked deep into my eyes so I would never forget what he was saying to me. 'The only important thing to know about God is that you are not He. Merely and magnificently a particle of God. Just stay grateful that you know you do not know – and even more grateful that you know you do not have to know, only to see, feel, and trust; and to practice, in both senses of the word.'

I sat down on a pew to the accompaniment of creaking wood. My eyes panned the scene. There was a sweet and sour taint of incense in the air. The church looked empty, except for an elderly, fragile-looking man who sat alone praying, his fingers locked into each other.

His words were clear.

'Thy command, that we may learn, even from them, hereafter to obey Thy name, for Thy mercy, in saving us, when we were ready to perish. Continue, we beseech thee, this Thy goodness to us.'

His presence, his faith moved me. I turned away, as if I were prying into his private world. I sat down, looked forward and noticed that ropes had been positioned down the aisles at the end of the hard, skinny pews. I presumed these were for blind people, to help them find their way to the altar.

I thought of my need to be guided. Then I noticed the priest, who was momentarily distracted by the slamming of a door. He took off his glasses, put them back on, and focused his gaze in my direction. I caught his stare and he immediately looked down. A warm breeze blew over me and a slight, thin figure appeared in the corner of my vision. Perhaps it was my imagination at that moment, or I was confused. Sweat was running from my forehead into my eyes. I was slightly brain damaged from the cumulative effects of the alcohol and other prerequisites of avoidance – and, don't let's forget, by grief.

'Excuse me. I hope I am not interrupting anything.'

It was the priest looking down at me.

'You wouldn't mind if I read you some passages I've been working on for Sunday?' he asked. 'It would be nice to get a little feedback.'

'Who me? Of course not,' I said, without thinking and without adding, 'Didn't you see I wanted to be alone?'

'I'll read it from here, if that's okay?' He sat in the pew directly ahead of mine rearranging himself to get comfortable. '… and the life of the world to come, so that this body may be made glorious, according to thy mighty working, whereby we are able to subdue all things to ourselves.'

His ecclesiastic presence surrounded me like a warm blanket. He seemed to understand, without me saying I longed to be anyone other than who I was; that I needed, or begged, for something that could help me move on, away from my pain. I felt like that monarch who would have willingly swapped his palace for a hermitage.

'Let us look at the past, yes, but not glare at it. Neither regret it nor shut the door on it.'

At that point I had nothing, nothing at all.

'Pray to acquire a better understanding,' he said, his tone changing from shrink to healer. 'Pray to understand how to cope with anything that crosses your path; or, at least, learn how not to add to your distress. For you, that sun is a little more dull today, although it will brighten tomorrow.'

Tears fell from my eyes.

The priest put his hand on my shoulder. He said nothing more.

∴

Intuitively I wanted to soak my body in water, perhaps subconsciously remembering that, in some religions, the worshippers wash thoroughly before any attempt is made to cleanse the soul.

I couldn't find my key. I pressed on the doorbell and pressed it again. I was in a hurry.

Lidia answered the door. She asked if I were okay.

'Can I get you anything?'

I shook my head and walked hurriedly upstairs. I went straight to the bathroom and immediately ran myself a bath. I stood there as it filled with water. I undressed and got into it, lay there stretched out, my knees like remote rocks in the middle of the ocean. The soap dish fell off the end of the bath, onto the surface of the water, transforming itself into a jet plane heading towards the rocks, experiencing a sudden tsunami (the movement of my body).

And then, everything was suddenly calmed. I was left lying in my bath quite still and silent, thinking my nightmares had to end. From now on, I would have to deal with my reality and celebrate my son's life. I reminded myself, the present can be stopped at any moment and a new future can begin. I decided, however it would be, I'd strive to recapture some joy and remember all the beauty I'd experienced: my first sight of the sunset, my first ever kiss, even the first taste of mustard.

Remember, acknowledge – and let go.

I wrapped a clean, white towel around my waist and looked deeply into the mirror. The dark lines under my eyes seemed to have lightened. My skin was giving off more colour. I decided to have a shave. I'd shaved only once in recent weeks. I didn't see the point in it. I was beginning to look like the bereted revolutionary portrayed on that student poster.

I dressed in different clothes from the ones I'd worn first thing that morning. I picked the first to hand from my row of shirts. As I put it on, I noticed it was a blue one given to me by Luke on my birthday. I didn't break down. I just smiled and started to pray. Yes, I prayed – if only for the time it takes a duellist to count his paces before turning. I prayed, not only because of what I'd experienced that morning, but because I no longer felt able to rely on my own strength. Anyway, as someone once said, the only people who scoff at prayer are those who have not tried it enough. I also no longer believed that, if my pain was ignored for long enough, it would eventually disappear.

So, that morning, I prayed for strength, compassion and understanding.

I needed to understand how the God I was turning to had given and taken away the most precious gift in my life.

∴

The black-and-white photograph had been left on the kitchen table. I tucked it into my shirt pocket without looking and made a promise that I would carry it always. Lidia had put together a salad to go with crusty bread and soup. I slurped it up without pause.

She looked at me, startled by my sudden fit of hunger. I looked back at her and took a deep breath. I hadn't noticed her pain; the constant weeping that had changed the shape of her face.

I suddenly remembered she'd known Luke all his life. She was here, the day we brought him home from the hospital – waiting just there, on the stoop outside, anxious to meet the new arrival.

I stood up, my face apologising for believing I was the only one suffering. I opened up my arms. I said I was so sorry.

And we hugged. Tightly.

Afterwards, I sat down and began to go through the rest of my post. The first envelope I came to had large, scribbled but legible letters. I stopped, pausing for thought. I opened it with a thumb and pulled out a handwritten letter, written in black ink.

It read:

March 21st, 1989

Dear Mr. Hammond,

I am Kate. My full name is Kate Louise Christina Penn.

I was Luke's girlfriend. The girl he was coming to see when his plane went down. The girl who planned to meet him at the airport carrying a silly balloon with the words 'Welcome to the Big Apple' written on it.

The girl who'd invited him to New York City to spend Christmas with her.

I knew immediately I'd fallen in love with your son, the minute we set eyes on each other. Momentarily, I felt like a victim plucked from the crowd by a knife thrower at the carnival. Why me? Why there, on that day, had my life changed?

And of course it did. It has, and will never be the same again. How I want to tell you how he was with me – the kindest and most decisive man I grew to know, who would bring me flowers in the morning. I once saw him hold up the traffic to help a blind man cross the road. At first, he was nervous to hold my hand as we walked together but then, slowly, I felt his grip more and more.

'I don't usually do this,' he once said. 'I'm not usually this open.'

He often spoke of you. His deep love and respect for his father. I wanted to meet you. But he said 'not yet'. Why? I'm not sure. Maybe you were his special prize to be revealed when the time was right. You see, we discussed getting married. Maybe we were too young, I thought.

'My Mum and Dad married at our age,' he told me, 'and they so loved each other.'

And now I don't have that choice. I'm sorry, I don't want to sound pitiful but I know I will regret forever the chance I missed. I so want to say, 'Yes, Luke, let's be together forever, for I never loved anyone like I love you' – but who would have known we had no time?

Perhaps one day you and I will meet, but for now (and I hope you understand), I have to mourn in peace. I don't have the strength to face you. Please, please do understand. I believe the only way I can survive is to store my precious memories away and gradually let them fall asleep forever, never allowing the cruelty of this world to disturb them.

Love from,
Kate

I shuffled in my chair. My breathing got heavier. The world went white. But what the morning had taught me was, I had the strength to face the shittiest shit of life, just by doing that: facing it.

I could stand in the deepest of water without moving. I didn't need to swim. By doing nothing, I could go with the flow, not fight anymore, hand everything over to a higher power, have faith to feel I'd reached a point near to understanding that concept of nothing. To have tasted a concept of everything.

I sat up with a jolt. I found a pen and paper, and I wrote a reply. I wrote quickly, leaning forward and mumbling to myself, marking each letter, each word with thick blue ink.

4th April 1989

Dearest Kate,

Hello. I am so happy and so sad to hear from you. Thank you for taking the time to write. Let me tell you what has been happening. Like you, I'm finding this difficult. I'm finding everything difficult. So, I am just going to put my head down and write.

If I ramble on or this letter becomes maudlin, I apologise.

I don't know whether you know, but miraculously Luke's body was found intact. In fact, he was one of the first to be discovered, probably while I was waiting for news at the nearby town hall. Nobody had the chance to warn me before a journalist banged on my door the following day, asking for a comment.

'This story will be splashed across the front pages, the weekly mags for weeks,' he boasted, licking his lips. 'The biggest tragedy of the century, worse than the Titanic!'

His aggression and lack of empathy were so appalling, his words only registered weeks later. It's been like that, my life full of noises I can't hear. My hands have stayed over my ears ever since.

We buried Luke in a grave close to where we live in London. The funeral was a small gathering, my choice, just family and close friends. I knew I couldn't bear to see the anguish on so many young faces, the curling of parents' arms round the shoulders of the young.

Perhaps I was being selfish. I'm not sure. I've noticed in my grief that what I believe in today, I may not believe in tomorrow.

I did try to reach out to you. Luke's best friend John – I understand you met him a number of times? – didn't have a contact number for you. Luke had promised to give it to me as soon as he arrived in New York. Please forgive me for not trying harder but I sense, from your letter, you wouldn't have wanted to be there.

The weather for the day of the funeral was fittingly miserable. It was bitter. My teeth chattered, my hands froze, even though I wore gloves. The fog cut straight through me. I wore Luke's very own black tie. The one he used to wear daily as part of his school uniform. As I was leaving the house, I suddenly remembered the tie and found it deep within his drawer. Quickly, I brushed it down with my hand, no time spent on ironing, and tied a knot the way he used to – a Windsor knot, as it is called.

As I looked in the mirror, I saw his face reflected back at me. I paused and smiled and then I stared a little longer and my face became ugly – a face so ugly, the craft that went into creating such snarls and knobs and chaotic angles became fascinating – and it was only my sister's voice that drew me away from my disturbing meditation.

I apologise if my honesty is hard to read, but I can only be honest at this time in my life.

I've been told there were fresh flowers in the chapel but I remember seeing nothing fresh, nothing beautiful. We sang the familiar sad hymns, our lips mouthing to the familiar words.

John read a eulogy. Our heads were bowed. It began with humour. Remembering how they first met in the schoolyard as seven year olds. How, that first morning, they began one of those mock fights in which one pretends to hit the other, while the other surreptitiously claps at the moment of impact, or holds up his hand to his face so that, to an observer, it is the face that is being hit and not the hand. And on that day, by chance or was it 'accidentally on purpose' – John let out a wide smile – Luke truly hit him in the face, and the fight suddenly turned real. I heard laughter. Genuine laughter, as we imagined Luke, who I know would have felt awful about it, trying to explain it was an accident.

'So we got ourselves into a fight the first time we met,' John continued. 'Here I was, meeting my best friend for the first time and we ended up wrestling to the ground.'

Then his tone changed. He recited that exquisite text that goes something like this:

Death is nothing at all. It does not count. I have only slipped away into the next room ... Life means all that it ever meant ... Why should I be out of mind because I am out of sight? I am but waiting for you, for an interval, somewhere very near, just around the corner. All is well ...'

He read the words with such beauty and dignity. I felt proud that he'd been Luke's best friend. He will grow into a fine man, someone this world will benefit from. Bless and protect him always.

My sister followed by reading the lesson, and another of Luke's friends sang a beautiful and melancholic song, the name of which I've forgotten. Yes, can you believe it? I'm sure I'll hear it again one day, when the universe decides I can withstand it. Astonishingly, applause broke out after he'd finished, sounding like reluctant rain, or the brief clapping of butterfly wings in the sun.

Probably those who clapped looked at it as a distraction from the pain of it all.

When we left the church and walked into the graveyard, the rain was unforgiving. The bells tolled, sounding muffled, like the scream of a train engine when the wind is coming from the other end of town.

Many of us slipped on the wet ground. My sister's husband and I shared an umbrella but I didn't care if I was getting soaked. I stood by the graveside, among craning necks and hearts trying to get a better view of something so horrible. The faces of my fellow mourners were ethereal. The priest threw pieces of earth onto the coffin. I had to be forcibly restrained from following my son as I watched the priest's fingers scattering that soil.

I admit it, with no shame. I didn't want to live any longer.

It was only today, a few hours ago to be precise, that I found a road that just might help silence my misery. I've never really prayed or gone to church, but the only hours since that dreadful day I've experienced any calm is when praying.

Oh, how wonderful it would be if I reached a stage of acceptance where prayer became part of my daily routine, like eating and sleeping, even breathing.

Do his murderers ever think, for one moment, about the sorrow they cause to so many? Do they consider the mental depths they fall into? Of course not, but they should. If only they could see the pain their actions caused to so many. Eventually, they'll meet their maker and justice will be served. I write this not just in hope, but also with conviction. Life cannot throw up such wickedness for there to be no reckoning.

This morning, I forced myself to go out for a walk. It wasn't long before I was passing my local church. I stopped and some force drove me inside. It wasn't an epiphany; it was a realisation that I needed help from a higher power. A priest sat beside me and tried to help with his words. I had a sense of gratitude for the first time in weeks. Don't they say gratitude alters attitude? Anyway, as I am writing, I remind myself that the majority of people will, in any case, at one time or another, have suffered, be about to suffer, or be suffering at this very moment at least one such tragedy on their journey through life. They also have their stories to tell.

I wanted to pass on to you what I experienced today. I hope you'll forgive me prattling on. With this letter, I'm enclosing a gift. I hope you won't mind. The day before Luke was going to fly to New York, I went out to buy him a present, something to keep him warm. I know how cold it gets in Manhattan. I found him a navy blue, polo neck cashmere sweater. However much I tried to give it to him, I somehow kept forgetting to.

Virtually his last words to me were, 'You can give it to me when I get back, it will still be cold.'

Anyway, I want you to have it. If you wish to give it away, please don't hesitate. If the sweater becomes a burden, get rid of it. It's yours and maybe it was always meant to be.

You wrote, 'I wish to mourn in peace.' It's strange because I uttered the same words this very morning, only a couple of hours before I opened your letter. So I understand you. I understand you well. This letter doesn't need a reply. It's simply an acknowledgment of yours.

To the girl my son loved. To the girl he was coming to see. I will let you mourn in peace, dear Kate.

Bless you,
Tom

I asked Lidia if there was a large envelope in the house. Before she could answer, I remembered there was one in the bottom of my desk. I pulled open the drawer, took out the envelope and folded the letter and the blue sweater.

It fitted into the envelope perfectly.

I copied Kate's address from her letter and wrote it down in block capitals, in a size that no one in the world could possibly misread.

'Just going to the post office!' I called out, and stepped onto the street.

There was suddenly nothing. No one, save the wind and a discarded newspaper flying down the road. I breathed deeply and sighed. I felt a little stronger. It was as if making contact with Kate had lifted something. I meant what I wrote. I'd leave her now, to get on with her life. She didn't need me to remind her of the pain. She'll have enough of that going on.

As I walked, I looked up to the sky. There was a flock of birds flying north, perfectly synchronised with each other. Yes, a flock of birds, which flew with such a miraculously unanimous instinct that anyone who claimed not to believe even in the concept of a God …

Was probably missing something important.

I bit my lip so as not to smile.

In the post office, I saw the envelope being thrown onto the 'air mail' pile. As it fell, I knew it was going to reach Kate. I had no doubt. I said goodbye. As I left, I took the black and white photograph out from my wallet and spoke it to it. It was becoming a habit to talk to Luke through it.

'I've sent the sweater. It's gone, Luke. She'll have it now. I promise you.'

V

The flat chose me. When I took my first steps inside, the door banged shut like a burst paper bag or more like a gunshot.

The sound represented a discord from my previous life. I felt a sense of relief. I'd put the house I'd shared with Luke and his mother on the market at the beginning of January, and thankfully it sold quickly. I couldn't bear to live there any longer. I sold my art, and most of my furniture. My new home was a good-sized, one-bedroom flat on the sixth floor of a wide, nine-floor Victorian building in Chelsea.

It was the first one I saw.

'I'll take it!' I said to the vendor.

The estate agent shook his head from side to side, like a metronome, with a finger waving to and fro in front of his mouth, meaning, 'You fool, let me deal with this' – but I wasn't interested in the long dance of buying a property. I had to get going, I was fidgety, there comes a moment in anyone's life when they're just tired and want to leave. However splendid the place and however much there is still to be seen, every beauty can come to look very like all the others.

Yes, that's how I felt, travelling along my road paved with deep regret. I thought about starting again in a different country, a different continent, but found myself unable to leave my neighbourhood.

It felt like I was taking part in a surrealist movie.

Those who talk of self-will are fooling themselves. Any plan, decision or action may seem to be the direct result of a will expressed, but who can know for sure they have control?

I was determined to cheer up – easy words to write or say out loud, but at that time it was a long, long road to reach any sort of optimism. I'd handed in my notice within a week of the new year starting. It was going to happen, wherever I'd been at the time.

The penultimate day of Luke's life was my last day in the financial world. I would never return to my desk. I asked Miss Varley to pack all my personal stuff and, when she had time, to taxi it over to me.

∴

When the doorbell rang one morning, I thought it was the Peter Jones department store delivering a new television. Instead, it was Miss Varley, standing beside two boxes – no hello, just, 'I thought I'd wait until you moved into your new home.'

Miss Varley had written a beautiful letter. She'd enclosed a pressed leaf from Primrose Hill, which she knew to be Luke's favourite park.

Sometimes it's the smallest things that have the greatest significance.

To connect with someone at this time must seem strange, not just to you. It does, it did, to me as well, but life can conjure up far from easy words like companionship, nature, affection, praise and, above all else – yes – love (or more precisely, the need to be in close physical contact).

I suppose in some way I was trying to learn the art of survival. I would say, in Miss Varley's defence, she didn't actively try to encourage my embrace. It was through her sweetness, her gentle words, that my breath was quite taken way.

She knew what I needed was a long and earnest kiss of life.

Yes, a kiss of life.

My gluttonous reaction was to feign near-death to be looked after, to be watched over. I needed someone. Our kissing, our touching, was awkward at first. We'd worked together for eight years, both concealing a shared desire, so it was never going to be smooth. When Miss Varley had fallen back towards me after spilling a glass of water, we both took the most of such an unexpected opportunity for two self- willed people to run a little riot, strangers next to each other in the back row of a movie house.

I can assure you this is all true. Although I wonder, not only whether this assurance is a sign of a troubled conscience still scared of thunder (which was, incidentally, rumbling and clapping, even exploding, outside) but also if it should even be necessary by this stage in my life. Why should I have to explain, justify or apologise for how I feel? How we felt? We can choose how we think, maybe better expressed as, 'We are not responsible for the thoughts that come into our heads, only for those we let stay there.'

But can I mould, manipulate, manage how I feel and conjure who I fall for?

Press the stop button on my fear, on my emotions, I thought. Because my son had died, I felt guilty for kissing and making love to a woman.

I was human, for God's sake. There. I said it.

I am human!

As Valerie fell onto the bed, I instinctively looked from side to side, as if to check no one was approaching and we were totally alone. After eight years of seeing each other virtually every day, we had changed moods – even personalities – with the speed of soap opera characters.

She didn't spend the day with me. I think we both suffered from the same unease. As I offered her the customary drink and cigarette afterwards, I asked, 'Is it alright if I call you Valerie?'

'You may,' she replied. 'Can I call you Tom?'

Ha! Talk about soap operas!

Before she left, she scribbled down her number, slowly, onto a piece of paper scented with lavender. The fragrance reminded me of countless memories from childhood, a time when my heart was at peace, I was breathing and managing my life with an assurance that anything threatening was safely hanging on a hook, like a winter coat.

∴

Valerie became a frequent visitor. One rule we agreed on was for her not to discuss work. I didn't want to hear or know any gossip about my former office. I realised, by setting that simple rule, I had no friends there, just acquaintances. Even that was pushing it. How sad – not unlike when you leave school and the group of friends you thought were inseparable from you turn out, in the real world, to be self-obsessed shits who don't listen to each other and ultimately couldn't give a fuck.

Friends. So few in life exist.

We never went out. Instead, I'd prepare dinner at home, working on an assortment of foods each day. Smoked salmon tucked into avocado; anchovies twirled around red hot peppers; artichoke hearts; pickled octopus in red wine. It was all food to dominate the taste buds. A meditative discourse in cooking.

Valerie only once critiqued my gastronomic prowess. After swallowing her lai chi floating in a sea of tomato juice, she grimaced.

'It's simply not to my taste!'

Poor thing. It did look like a large globule of bright goo floating about in a sea of blood. She probably hated everything I prepared, but she said nothing. Afterwards, we'd watch whatever movie was on TV. I noticed, when something sad happened, she would grab hold of my hand and squeeze it.

'Please don't do that,' I wanted to say. But I knew she meant well and I don't think I had the strength to fight. I don't like to fight but, when she'd had too much to drink, I'd slump in quiet resignation and listen to her warbling.

'You are as happy as you make your mind up to be,' she said, with a mock wagging of a finger.

Yes … yes … yes …

It would go on, until her voice crashed into the midriff of my brain and we'd start yelling at each other. We were both at a point in our lives that made quarrels unavoidable.

We decided, after three weeks of squabbling, to take a break from each other. Valerie took a holiday with a couple of girlfriends, a week in Faro. I was surprised to find I missed her company. I spent too much time alone. Yet, no sooner had she returned, we began sniping at each other again, and the same evening performances took place.

There was the never-empty glass of scotch.

'Just a wee bit more,' she would say, in a mock Scottish accent.

And then there was her repetitive use of hackneyed arguments.

'There is no gain without pain.'

I was told I had an inability to be sweet, kind, understanding.

'How can I?' I'd argue. 'I can't even be that to myself.'

Silence followed by silence, until she felt the need to disturb it and then she talked straight at me, without pause, until she said something that hurt.

'I was only joking! What I really meant was …'

And then, instead of dropping the subject, she'd try to explain that she meant nothing by it; try to cover up; wriggle herself out of the situation. Eventually she tied herself into asphyxiating knots and I laughed, in that dismissive fashion, which would make her feel like shit until she'd stand up, eyes front and start to leave.

'Come back,' I'd say weakly, followed by my turn to say, 'I didn't mean it.'

At first, she didn't react. She'd be halfway down to the street before I caught up with her and led her back. Then she would quickly sober up and, in her seduction, undo a third button on her shirt to reveal her beautiful breasts with a mischievous grin on her face, a twinkle in the eye, a flutter in her fingers that would have made an observer guess that she indulged in nefarious practices.

I groped, fondled and squeezed. At last I found myself touching her chest. I pulled open her shirt with the same passion as on the very first night we spent together. Yes, with the passion of someone who'd wanted her for years.

I didn't sleep well on the night she returned from her Portuguese holiday. A pulse had started to vibrate in my left gum, just above the wisdom tooth. It felt as if I were being poked by an alcoholic dentist, prodding at my teeth with his probe before he'd had sufficient whisky to calm his shakes. My graph of tolerance was low, that of my irritability high. And climbing.

I looked across at Valerie, who was sleeping soundly. Poor Valerie, who hadn't stood a chance. I recognised I was numbly incapable of appreciating anything. I didn't even recognise she felt sorry for me. Poor Valerie, meanwhile, wasn't strong enough to deal with her own cocktail of drink and insecurities, and my grief as well.

To be fair, it must have been a near-impossible task.

As I listened to her gentle snoring, transfixed by her twitching lips, I concluded that something momentous had happened earlier in her life, from which she hadn't yet fully recovered and probably never would. Having accepted this last fact, however, she could now smile her way through most problems, even catastrophes, because anything else was, in comparison, as insignificant as those peanuts in the bowl she sweetly bought for me.

Why, you fool, I thought. *Stop judging and making your life even more difficult.*

I got out of bed, took one look at the world outside, went back to bed, slept, woke, spent the next hour thinking of a strong enough reason to get up, slept again, and received my just desserts: after the dreams came the nightmares. Giant creepy-crawlies that bred in the walls of the flat and now writhed, in slow motion, seeking to contact the light. Soon they surrounded me and began to cover my body. Some of them began to gnaw into my skin. I was faced with a situation so life-like, I actually felt the pain of my skin being pulled apart, and looked down to see my cadaverous ribcage packed with giant insects, black mambas and solifugae.

I was woken by a sudden noise coming from the kitchen. A pile of Luke's magazines, which I was in the process of organising, had fallen to the floor.

'Hey, I'm still alive! I'm here! In my room. In my bed,' I said out loud.

I shushed myself and crept into the bathroom to have a shower. I was evidently still nervous because, as I was soaking myself with steaming water, I kept the shower curtain wide open. Just in case a psychopath chose to creep up on me.

I picked up the magazines, drank a glass of orange juice and decided to get out and have some fresh air.

The streets were beginning to stir but again I was lost in my thoughts looking at the buildings while trying to determine what their original and subsequent occupants thought, felt, dreamed or feared. I spoke to the ground I walked upon to ask about the souls that had previously stepped on those stones. All these rants reassuring me that I was getting closer to the answer, to the why?

It wasn't too far from my flat that I walked by a small precinct of shops. A sign 'FOR LEASE' hung outside one with a large bay window. It used to be a health food shop, but was now empty. I peered into an empty space. All that remained was a Yellow Pages that lay forlornly in the middle of the floor. The shop was a good size, both in width and depth.

I paused and thought for a moment, *I used to be indecisive but now I'm not so sure.*

Ha! I threw away the quote and found a telephone in the nearby coffee bar to dial the estate agent whose name was on the board. Too early, it went straight to an answering machine. I didn't leave a message. Instead, I promised myself I would call back, which I did, at precisely nine o'clock. By nine-thirty, the agent had arrived with a set of keys.

As he walked towards me, he extracted from his top pocket a pair of sunglasses, although it was a grey and forlorn morning or perhaps only appeared to be so to me, being merely a reflection of my restless night.

'Sorry about these,' he said pointing to the dark glasses, 'I've a splitting headache.'

He spoke facing one direction and yet I'm sure his pupils had swivelled to the building he was about to show. It was all very disconcerting. As soon as he opened the door, he started to sell it.

'Please be quiet,' I said, 'I'd prefer to walk through and value it myself and in silence.'

Pompous or what? But I felt excited.

Yes. It was perfect.

This is going to be my bookshop!

By the time we'd walked to his car, we'd shaken on the deal.

He promised the papers would be biked over for signature that very morning.

'Good doing business with you,' he said.

'And with you,' I said. 'But, before you go, a word of advice. If you don't face reality with natural eyes and only wear those dark glasses when the sun is out, you can imagine that the worst is about to happen, when it isn't necessarily going to. I remember one of my favourite great-aunts being seen to carry in all the deckchairs from the garden on a bright day. She did it because she'd woken suddenly and thought, because of seeing through her sunglasses, that rain was on its way.'

He took off the glasses, squinted his eyes and looked confused.

'But sir, it is the brightest of days.'

I looked up at the sky and it was as clear as crystal. I let it fill my eyes with its wonder. For the first time in months I didn't need to comprehend that unanswerable question of why.

∴

Before returning home, I decided to pay a visit to the church, to thank God for guiding me to a new chapter. I pushed at the door but it was locked. I pushed again. No, it was bolted. How ridiculous. I sat on the stoop and waited for it to open. I noticed then, in the gutter, empty bottles and cigarette packets; crumpled pages from notebooks; a discarded sandwich; and, torn-up sheets of a screenplay.

I closed my eyes and tried to meditate by concentrating on the very tip of my nose, breathing slowly and regularly, first through my mid-forehead, then my heart, then my stomach.

Courage! Wisdom!

I'd been to a meditation class the week before, hoping to blank out everything and everyone when they called upon me uninvited. The following day, though, when I visited the priest, he advised me to keep my heart open, to not shut out anyone or anything.

'That is the journey to true healing.'

And here I was. Stood waiting outside a locked church. I was always taught that a locked door meant there was something inside worth having. Anyway, I was sure the higher power wouldn't mind losing a few silver cups or a little defecation in the aisle. I wasn't going to wait any longer. I got up and dusted down my clothes. I didn't need a crucifix to focus my mind. Instead, I started to stage-whisper a verse from *Ode to a Nightingale*. I'd studied the poem at school; it had always meant so much to me, but it wasn't until that moment I truly realised why.

Now more than ever seems it rich to die,
To cease upon the midnight with no pain,
While thou art pouring forth thy soul abroad
In such an ecstasy!
Still wouldst thou sing, and I have ears in vain –
To thy high requiem become a sod.

∴

I saw a hoarding with a sign, 'BEWARE OF MISGUIDED LOVE', and a picture of that marathon runner being helped across the line so that, although first to arrive, he was disqualified.

Misguided love is better than no love at all, isn't it?

I stopped off at *The Markham Arms* and bought myself a drink. The barman eyed me cautiously, as if he knew there was something unsavoury about me; or, perhaps, I had a rather large pimple on the end of my nose that made looking at me disagreeable.

Whatever it was, I didn't care.

I sat in the corner of the pub. I felt better. Better than I thought I ever would. Yes. Better. A little better. I gulped down my vodka and took the black and white photo from my pocket.

'Hey Luke, you said to open a bookshop, one I've always dreamed of. And look, my darling boy! I've found it. Thank you for guiding me there.'

∴

The lease, as promised, arrived by courier. I signed it. The fear was creeping back into my life. I felt if I didn't sign immediately, I'd miss out. I wasn't willing to take that chance.

It was time for a celebration. I hadn't been out for months, not since – well, not since that night. Luke's godfather, Jack Fitzroy, had sent an invitation for his fiftieth birthday celebration. At first, I'd ignored it. He wouldn't take no for an answer, though, and followed it up with a series of phone calls. I'd invent a hundred excuses, until one day my imagination ran dry.

I simply said to him, 'I just don't have the strength to face anyone.'

'Not to worry. If you change your mind, just turn up. There's no need to call.'

Dear Jack. A good friend known for his generosity, dedication to his work and the warmest of hearts. The sort no one and nothing can blow out or blow away.

I called Valerie to ask whether she'd like to come to Jack's party.

She was surprised by the upbeat sound of my voice. 'Yes please,' she said.

'I'll pick you up at eight o'clock, then.'

Just as I was about to replace the receiver, I heard her say something.

'But you don't have my address.'

She was right. In all the time we'd been seeing each other, I hadn't once visited her home, nor even bothered to ask where she lived.

∴

My car was filthy. I hadn't driven nor gone anywhere near it since coming down from Scotland. I'd promised myself for weeks that I'd clean out the empty bottles of water and old sandwich wrappers, but I hadn't. I couldn't even bear the thought of hearing the sound of the engine, or finding the same radio station I'd left it on when I parked up.

I'd thought of just giving the car away but had never got round to it.

When I sat in front of the steering wheel, I took a deep breath and slammed the side door shut, hard. I paused and started to drum the gear stick with my fingers, not only with zest but a certain rhythm. I felt my emotions soaring and plummeting dramatically. I was about to start the engine, but then I hesitated.

'Come on,' I said to myself, 'move your life forward.'

I turned the ignition.

Not a sound. Except, perhaps, a very soft clicking, as of a clock. Was my imagination deceiving me, my ears hearing sounds from my subconscious? I could have sworn I detected some deep grunts, as if someone had been gagged and was now being subjected to great pain. I shook my head and turned the key once again. This time it started without hesitation, with the radio up on high volume. Yes – on the station I'd left it tuned to, months before. I quickly turned the dial and found the faint sound of Frank Sinatra singing 'dobody do' as if he was singing through shower room steam. I looked at my watch and without another thought drove off, stopping to get fuel before picking up Valerie. I piled up the rubbish and threw it into a bin on the forecourt. I then went through the carwash and, by the time I drove into Valerie's rather drab terraced street, the car looked as good as new.

She was waiting. I saw her face looking out from a chink of light shining from a drawn curtain. For a second, the light blinded my eyes, scorched each nerve ending, searing me from head to heart, gut to feet. I felt I was on a date.

I was about to ring the doorbell when she opened the door.

'You look a picture tonight,' I said, sounding like a sugar daddy.

'Thank you,' Valerie replied. 'But, what sort of picture? There are some pretty ugly ones around, you know. I've heard, or read somewhere, that the ugliest can seem beautiful if kept for long enough on a familiar wall.'

My ex-secretary sounded as if she was trying to regain her form.

∴

'Ah good, you made it – come here!' Jack pulled me to his chest and gave me a tight hug. He glanced at Valerie, who was standing beside me like an obedient schoolgirl. 'And who do we have here?'

'This is Valerie Varley.'

'How do you do?' Jack said, and paused for a moment. 'Not the same Valerie Varley that worked for you?'

He gave an ill-timed laugh, the only purpose of which, I deduced with paranoia, was to benefit an unseen audience.

'The very same one,' I answered.

'Well, well, well. We've never met.' Jack noticed my left eyebrow rise but ignored it. 'We've spoken on the phone at least a hundred times over the years. Wow, you are very pretty!'

'Care for a drink?' I interrupted, virtually pushing Valerie away.

'Thank you,' Valerie replied, looking at the makeshift bar with disconcerting keenness.

Jack gave me a discrete thumbs-up and I stole a smile, from whom I'm not sure.

It was a big jump to go out and confront friends. I was like a person who's made a great decision and expects all the changes to come at once. Abracadabra and hey presto! I heard fringes of gossip from the guests as we made our way to the bar. Their voices clashed with the live band tuning up – or were they playing? I had to imagine some ends of sentences, and fill in the gaps.

Valerie asked for a whisky, so I decided to join her. I downed it one. Yuck! As I was doing so, I felt the eyes of the room watching my every move.

Let's have another.

The second went down just as easily as the first …

Valerie was already on her third. I took the drink from her hand.

'Come on, let's dance,' I said.

Before she could answer, I was gyrating across the dance floor. Poor Valerie was desperately trying to follow my steps. Jack came to her rescue and took her by the hand.

'Don't mind me butting in, do you?' he boomed.

I didn't. The floor had begun to roll like a ride at a funfair.

I headed straight to the bathroom and put my head under cold running water. I looked in the mirror. What a sight! And I was feeling so happy, let's say so much better, a few hours earlier. I just needed a little alcoholic help.

Oh God, please don't let me be sick …

I crouched down on my knees and started to take slow breaths. I allowed my eyelids to fall and then opened them again. I took a deep, deep breath.

Ah, that's better. A little better.

Prayers work. Yes.

Keep praying. Pray until something happens!

Soon, I was back in the party, shaking hands with friends. Each and every one of them passed on their condolences, no fear in doing so, just empathy for my pain, my loss. Valerie was no longer dancing, instead talking quietly but enthusiastically to a handsome man. He was holding a bottle of blood-red wine in one hand, an empty glass in the other.

'Like a drink?' he asked, in an over-familiar tone, thrusting the bottle into my hand.

'No, thanks. I think I've already had enough.'

'Everything all right?' Valerie asked.

I nodded and made the excuse that I needed to go off and talk to someone. She got up to follow.

'No, I'd better go alone. It's rather p-private,' I stuttered, signalling her to continue with her conversation.

'Nice suit,' the handsome man said.

Oh no. I recognised that sort of creepy flattery.

I faked a smile and moved away.

Oh dear, I was not in a good state. Maybe I was feeling jealous? Yes, jealousy crawls all over friendship, joy, and health, even life itself. Maybe I didn't have the strength to deal with any emotions other than grief.

Just as I was about to walk outside to get some fresh air, a hand touched me on my shoulder. I was shocked, as if something had brushed against me like in a Ghost Train ride but then, thinking it might be someone's idea of a joke – i.e. you touch someone on one shoulder but you're standing by his other – I turned around.

'Hi!' a woman said.

'Hello.'

'You don't recognise me, do you?'

I shook my head.

'It's Julia.'

Of course it was Julia. My wife's closest friend.

Still ravishing, still beautiful like a silver screen movie star.

'Were you heading somewhere?' she asked.

'I just needed some air.'

'Come on then.'

She took my hand and led me outside, where we both leaned against a wall. She lit a cigarette. She looked and she listened as I spoke of Luke, breathing in the smoke that became progressively more complex as each minute passed, as if the inhalation of it represented a soft padding of a troubled brow, while at the same time pre-empting the hammerings of distant nails into unseen coffins.

The air suddenly turned chill. Another plume of smoke drifted from Julia's mouth. She flicked at least a third of her cigarette to the ground. It was still burning.

'It's getting cold. Let's get back inside,' she said. 'I'll find somewhere to sit and you get the drinks.'

So, up I went to the bar and looked at the bottles neatly lined up on the table. I wasn't sure if it was a good idea to have another drink – not after my near-collapse in the bathroom – but, other than the whisky, I felt strong enough to try something.

'What would you like?' asked the student barman.

'I'll have two of whatever the person lying on the floor's having,' I said.

The barman duly handed me two glasses of brandy. As I carried them over to Julia, I turned and saw Valerie still in full flow with Mr Handsome. She blew me a kiss and then continued talking with her new friend.

I could see her eyelashes flutter, like a hummingbird's wings.

Julia beckoned me. 'Do you come here often?' she asked, jokingly.

'No. I usually prefer to drink alone, that way I don't bother anyone,' I replied flippantly, remembering how we used to joust with each other.

'I still have that picture of Luke taken shortly after Kate died. Do you remember it was early evening in Regent's Park? The ducks crowding round us in hope of food, and you snapping away with your new camera? Ha! You took one step back and fell into the lake. You got absolutely soaked! Do you remember, Tom? Do you remember?'

We laughed at our shared memory and, as Julia squeezed my hand, I felt a shimmer of something.

Silence spoke its golden volumes, only broken by me saying, 'I now carry a photo of Luke everywhere, taken on the last night of his life. Do you know it's the only photo I have of the two of us?'

I took the photograph out of my pocket and handed it to her.

She looked, at first, to be acting out a skill of looking without looking. But then, her head started to sway a little and she wept for me, for the loss of my son and the memory of her best friend.

'I'm so sorry,' she said and stretched her hand towards mine.

Suddenly, Valerie came up to the table.

Julia quickly pulled her hand away.

Valerie, flushed, had too much to drink. She was downcast and curt.

I stood up as if guilty of something.

'Valerie, Julia; Julia, Valerie. Food, anyone?'

I moved away without hearing an answer. I passed the live band. They seemed unsure what to play, strumming a rumba that transformed into a sort of pavane and finally into a reggae version of *Happy Birthday.*

A voice beside me soared an octave, until presumably his wife slapped the back of his head. Balloons fell from a hanging net and the party started in unison to cheer and stamp on the balloons. Valerie led the way, jumping down with both feet and pushing anyone and everyone out of her way. Her behaviour was out of control. Or was it? Perhaps she was just having a good time but I felt like hiding my face in my hands.

Jack blew out the candles and before we could all join together in a verse of *For He's a Jolly Good Fellow*, Miles (an old school friend) pounced and started to make an 'I'll be brief ' speech which would carry on for eternity. He was the sort of person who'd take a long pause between each sentence, expecting his audience to react. We didn't. We'd heard it all before, played in numerous keys and orchestrations.

He spoke the syllables pizzicato.

'We have shared the most wonderful of holidays together,' he hurried on, as if even he was starting to feel the need for some forward movement through the sludge. Then, without warning, he changed his voice into a minor key, as if what he was about to say was much more worthy of being heard than everything that had gone before. Admittedly, it was not that difficult. 'I met my wife at Jack's villa in Cap Ferrat,' he said. 'And I thought, as we frolicked by the pool, what a lucky chap I am and what a jolly good fellow Jack is …'

This mention of his wife seemed to make him splutter, perhaps at the realisation that no way would his wife be able to ever revisit those halcyon days of bikinis and a lithe body.

'Now, there are one or two other things I would like to mention …'

And on he went. And on. And on …

I began to reckon I would cut the passage right there, before I considered cutting his throat or my wrists – then and there and again, right now, in the telling of it, the memory. Valerie was clapping loudly at every lame joke, encouraging the bore to continue. I was embarrassed, impatient and angry: another bad mixture. But, if I'm honest, another part of me began to find itself mollified, almost anaesthetised by the whole event.

I caught sight of Julia's gaze. She saw how I was feeling.

'I'm going,' she mouthed and pointed to the door.

Ah, how I wish I could go with her.

When Miles finished at last and Jack got round to thanking everyone for coming, Valerie was swaying backwards and forwards, grabbing mechanically at a table to find her balance. At one point, she was about to collapse, until I grabbed her by the elbow and led her outside.

'I'd better take you home,' I said, letting go of her elbow.

Her face hardened. 'You're embarrassed to be seen out with me,' she yelled.

I instantly rebutted her. 'Like this I am!'

In truth, though, she wasn't wrong. I wasn't ready to be out with anyone.

The drive home was theatrical, especially when Valerie took out her handkerchief and instead of dabbing her tears, fashioned it into a noose, pulled it tight and threw it into my chest.

I think she half-expected me to burst into applause.

I increased my speed. I wasn't ready to fight. Maybe it would've been better if I had. When we reached her house, I got out and went round to open the car door.

She wouldn't move.

'Sleep off your drink and I will call you in the morning,' I said.

She shook her head, crossed her arms and clicked the lock, then laughed at my face through the glass. She looked at me with crazed eyes.

I began to see what I could not see.

I went back to my side of the car, unlocked the door and reached across, pushing her out.

She asked me to stay. I declined.

The door slammed her out of my car and out of my immediate life, perhaps forever. My eyes followed her as she staggered, reluctantly, into her house.

'I'm sorry!' I shouted after her. 'I just don't have the strength to deal with this.'

I didn't want to hurt anyone, especially someone who was hurting herself.

She never called, not once. I never by chance ran into her again. Looking back, I've always been grateful that she showed me affection at a time when, without me knowing, I needed it more than ever.

Reaching home, I hesitated, switched off the engine and sat in the car. I focused my eyes on a streetlamp and thought I saw Luke's face or another known face; some face with a familiar, friendly smile. An honest face. I felt numb. I even thought, for one shivery moment, that I heard Luke's voice.

'Is that you, Luke?' I called out.

There was no answer. The roads were deserted, curtains drawn at every house.

I started up the car and drove slowly through London, passing no one. A half- drizzle had begun to come down and there was a hint of mist, clouding all details. I kept driving.

I knew exactly where I was heading.

As I approached the familiar street, the rain gathered just like it had done on the penultimate night of Luke's life. I drew up to the building where the bingo party was held only months before. I looked up at a clock just above the door. It had stopped – if it had even started – by coincidence at the exact time we'd left the party. I didn't think too much of this. Coincidences were happening with increased frequency, like that afternoon when I signed the lease: the same road where my new shop was got a mention on the local radio station. It can be exciting and disconcerting to be thinking, saying, even writing, a word, when the same word is heard on the radio or TV or across a room. It's exciting because the odds against it are so long, like your chances of winning the lottery. It's disconcerting because it makes me think it's not a coincidence at all, instead suggesting there may be more serious influences around and about and ahead.

I got out of the car and stood in the rain. It sounded like applause.

'Let the rains bedraggle me out of recognition!' I shouted. 'Long live this storm!'

Just like my son on this same street three months earlier.

I was starting to look like a bedraggled, storm-struck scarecrow. Sheet lightning, so rare in the city, lit up the street with no accompanying thunder. I must've been there for hours because, by the time I decided to return to my car, the dawn was breaking. The first jet of the day was crossing the sky on its way to Heathrow.

The seat groaned as I sat on it in my wet clothes. The smell of my wet jacket filled the car. I cupped my hands and cackled at the madness my grief had introduced to my life.

I have to be alone now to deal with the future. No distractions or I won't survive.

V

I needed to mourn in my own peace. I'd walk to my bookshop with the imaginary sound of waves making their way towards a pebbled shore. Throughout my life, I'd been in search of a job that would give me a certain stillness. I knew Luke wanted it for me. I hoped, in my darkest days, I might have found it at last.

VI

The policeman listened carefully. He took out a pen and notebook from his inside pocket.

'The photograph was taken a long time ago. Twenty-four years ago, to be exact. It's of a handsome young man in his early twenties, wearing a double-breasted dinner jacket, dressed in a black bow tie. His arm is wrapped around my shoulder.'

He was scribbling down what I was saying.

'The young man is my son.'

He raised his eyebrow. 'And where is he these days?' he asked jovially.

'He's no longer alive. He was murdered a day after the photograph was taken.'

'I'm s-s-sorry,' he stuttered, and immediately stopped writing.

His awkwardness, the way he fumbled with his notebook, his change of expression, reminded me of how people were when they ran into me shortly after Luke had been murdered.

The sudden hush at the chance meeting, the scene falling as quiet as the pushing of a pen, intensified by what they wanted to say and what I thought – at that time anyway – I didn't want to hear.

'We will do our very best to recover it – the photograph – I mean, everything: the bag, money, keys … Everything.'

'It's the only photograph I have of the two of us together. Since his death, every day, I've carried it with me.' I pointed to my heart, where the inside pocket of my jacket fell. 'Usually here. But, because of the heat today, I put it in the bag.'

'Can't you get a copy?' he asked softly.

'I tried a few months back to get the negative when I read the photographer's obituary in *The Times*. I hadn't thought of it before. Stupid, of course. So, I called his studio asking if it was possible. Someone called back to say they couldn't find anything from that particular evening. I should've thought to scan it, long ago. I never did.'

I felt a jolt as I thought of the photograph, like rummaging through a chest of drawers and coming across a faded message, letter, postcard or, indeed, a photograph. We look at the writing, at the face and remember the person. Then we pause and remember them a little bit more.

I recalled how Luke looked that night: his slightly embarrassed expression when the camera flashed; how he carried a smile 'as brief as a flash of sunlight caught on the porthole of a faraway ship, or on a spider's web swaying in the breeze' ...

Professor Keys interrupted the silence with his daily visit to the bookshop.

'Well, I'd better be going,' the policeman said, in his best voice that came with a thrill and a trill. He looked suspiciously into Professor Keys' eyes and wished us both a 'good day.'

The professor, a retired surgeon, was wearing his cap, which he always did. He said it gave him a sense of authority. He was a very clean man, probably a hangover from back when he scrubbed his hands each time he finger-tipped another human. His aftershave even had a faint scent of formaldehyde. He never said 'hello' or 'how are you?' but instead would go straight into a story.

Generally these stories included himself but he probably wasn't really in them, or thought it added a bit of spice to feature himself. I've heard such stories referred to as urban myths or, better, modern fairy tales or, best, my cousin stories. The narrator assures us it was his cousin who was involved, yet we hear the same story time and again, from different people, in various forms.

Before he delved into his latest yarn, I asked Professor Keys a question.

'Professor, you wouldn't mind watching the shop for me? I've something I need to do.'

Before he had time to answer, I walked out onto the street. A haze now covered the sun, which meant the temperature was lower now than the intense heat of only a few hours before. The air had cooled, not much.

Hannah was serving outside and gave me a wave.

A wind burst by, as if urging me to keep moving. I was heading towards my local church, the same one I'd visited on the morning I got the letter from Kate in New York. The same morning I'd become a little stronger. The same day I knew I could continue. The same day I believed in a higher power that could guide and perhaps carry me through the worst of my troubles and worst of my days.

∴

I had to cut through a small park to reach the church. The weather had encouraged the pale to lie out in front of the sun, some of them evidently having been tanning for too long. The deckchairs had been ungagged and a man in uniform was issuing tickets.

My, his job must have been part-time. How many sunny days were there in a year? That said, the good weather was heading into its fifth week, the tabloids challenging their subs to come up with new headlines more original than *PHEW WHAT A SCORCHER!*

I noticed the deckchairs had numbers inscribed on them, where loungers were most likely to catch their fingers.

I looked at the number nearest to me.

Clickety click! Sixty-six – Luke's winning number – BINGO!

Yes, the memories and coincidences kept following me …

The park attendant, who was dressed in a starched blue uniform, watched as those with chairs put coins into the cash box. He issued each of them with a ticket, not unlike a London bus conductor. He seemed a little out of place, in much the same way as uniformed police officers sometimes do in a local pub.

No one seemed to care. The local council wasn't going to miss the chance of some extra cash. I passed a husband reading his paper, taking a bite from his sandwich as his wife has trouble rearranging her deck chair.

'Can I help, dear?' he asked, sounding as if that was probably the last thing he wanted to do. What he really meant was, 'Could you get on with it, so I can read my paper in peace?'

Another picked up his chair and moved it to a position where he could observe those playing in the fountain and be in the shade. An oak tree provided perfect cover for when the sun became too intense. He ham-fistedly tried to unravel his chair.

Then I heard someone laughing. I wasn't sure who he was laughing at because, as I turned to face him, he turned away. I looked around the park one more time and watched a couple of kids enjoying themselves in a game of leapfrog, treading that dividing line between playing and fighting.

I smiled at the joy of being young again, of how much life has to offer.

I was jolted out of my trance by a conversation between two old women. One of them, wearing wire-rimmed glasses, said rather too loudly, 'A young death is more difficult to cope with, simply because it points to what might have been rather than what was …'

'Yes. A half-finished building, never to be finished, is more tragic than an old one falling down,' the friend concurred. 'Take me, for instance. If I dropped dead tomorrow, I'm sure you and maybe a couple of others would be sorry but I doubt there'd be much regret.'

The first woman's expression changed. 'Don't talk nonsense, my dear. Who the hell would I be able to moan to?'

The sound of a radio trying to pick up a station snapped me out of my eavesdropping. I quickly walked away.

The church resembled a building in a theme park that was supposed to have opened today but would instead open tomorrow. A string of lights were being hung above its entrance and the gardener was painting out the words 'Summer Fete' onto what looked like a strip of sailcloth. He gave me a cheerful hello and started to flay with his paintbrush at several wasps that had begun to circulate around his head. There weren't enough to call it a swarm but there must've been at least twelve – certainly enough for me to stop and advise him to calm down and walk away.

He did exactly that. Before I went into the church, I noticed the wasps had resumed their manic course and were bothering someone else. Inside, it was far busier than one might imagine for midday on a Tuesday in the heart of summer. The priest was showing schoolchildren around the church. Hardly a word of his well-rehearsed banter could be heard, however much he shouted, because the choir was rehearsing with a new sound system. The microphones were turned up too high, the feedback helping to create, not the sound of angels, but a variety of roars, hissings and throbbings.

'Even God might not be able to hear our prayers today,' remarked a stranger as I crossed myself.

'What do you say?'

'I don't think even if I screamed I could be heard …'

The stranger screamed at the exact same moment the sound system cut off. This caused the choir to stop singing, and the priest and schoolchildren turned to look.

'Oh dear,' the stranger meekly said.

I sat in the middle pew and now it was my turn, the words thundering out.

'God!' Pause. 'Oh, most powerful God! As I understand thee, why is this happening? What have I done to deserve this?'

I stopped shouting and looked up into the roof of the spiral. It was a mess of colours: rhubarb reds and pewter greys; purples and cinnamon; electric blues, only faintly saddened by my eyes focusing on a thin line of black on a small ledge, like the signature on the envelope of a mourning letter announcing the death of someone.

I shouted again. 'God, are you listening?'

Hearing and seeing an older man yelling must have been a fright for the schoolchildren. It's hard enough for the young to believe the elderly are emotionally alive, let alone capable of outbursts. One of the children turned towards me, and laughed.

I wasn't sure what he was laughing about. Embarrassment, probably.

I turned to find the priest. His face had the kindest of expressions, as if it were tailor-made for this very situation.

'I'm all ears should you need to talk to anyone,' he said, sounding more like a talk-show host than a priest. 'The children are about to be collected, then I'll be free. Why don't you stay here a while and we could have a little chat?'

I didn't answer. He was right. I needed to talk. I'd become used to the side that wanted to be alone, unable to cope with anybody, including myself. Maybe the gentle loss of memory and imaginary voices was God's grace, letting me go.

The priest, true to his word, came to sit next to me. It wasn't long before I was talking about death and the concept of an afterlife; how I'd been at a dinner party where our host spoke about it for most of the evening.

'It's a huge lie invented by those who want to make sure they have dominion over us in this life, this idea that there must be something more than mere existence, otherwise there'd be no purpose behind all the kerfuffle of creation. The universe originated in a cipher, and aimlessly rushes nowhere.'

Strange. Friends used to talk about the arts to deflect self-pity but now they talk about death.

The priest stared at me from a couple of inches away.

'Shall we talk about you for a moment?' he asked, breaking from my theme of death.

I told him about the robbery earlier in the day. I could smell his breath, which was surprisingly fresh. Peppermint. I contemplated how this random act of theft had put me in a tailspin; how it felt like the panic of running downhill, out of control, that scary moment when the hill takes over and I'm heading towards the precipice to topple over, be sucked into the brine.

'I asked God to give me back my photograph. It's just too painful. That's why I shouted, so God can hear my anguish.'

Each and every word.

'I've been coming here ever since I lost my son. I've never doubted. My faith gave me strength to go on. I've found comfort in my belief. But now? I can't understand why a higher power would allow something like this to happen.'

The priest set his hand on top of mine.

I released an honest threat. 'If my photograph isn't returned, I'll take my last breath on this earth not believing there is a God, believing instead that my life has been wasted in the hours I've spent here.'

I looked up at the cross and at the stained glass windows around the building that once seemed to me like the peaceful lake at the edge of a loud and manic city.

The priest said, 'He is listening.'

He left me alone. In my loneliness I tried to meditate, to mediate those games in my mind; to pacify the ache pulsing in my head; to mollify, even pamper, the soul.

I just sat and thought and then I thought, *Sometimes I just sit. Sometimes I lie and think.*

And then I thought, *Sometimes I just lie.*

'O most mighty and gracious God as we understand thee ...'

∴

When I left the church, I noticed the park was still full. A small child threw his ice cream cone to the ground. A few drops of it splattered onto my jacket. His parents seemed not to notice, let alone care.

His eyes said sorry.

'Don't worry,' I whispered.

I stopped off at the ice cream stall and asked for a paper napkin. It was given to me without a word and I joined the line for the water fountain. I always thought queues were a good barometer for moods. So, as I stood and waited, I noticed my uneasiness.

When I finally reached the fountain, I dampened the end of the napkin and dabbed the stains away.

'At least it's not vomit,' the person standing behind me said.

I sort of laughed, at the ridiculousness of the statement.

'Thank you,' I said, smiling and clenching my teeth at the same time. 'Can't stop, I'm afraid.'

The church bells began to chime the hour. I realised I'd been in the church for some time. I wasn't at all sure if Professor Keys would still be minding the shop. I had my doubts. But, to my surprise, he was waiting outside in the street, furtively glancing at his watch. When he saw me approaching, his face began to redden like a sunrise.

'Sorry I took a bit longer than I thought I would,' I said, shamefully.

He was in no mood to hear excuses. 'I simply didn't know what had happened to you. I understand you had a robbery this morning, so the last thing I was going to do was leave the store unattended. I mean really, what sort of behaviour is this? I had an important lunch to get to.'

Now his neck had also turned red. He was right and I was wrong. But then he adopted a more pugilistic approach, dancing in the middle of the ring as it were, putting out a few short jabs.

'Who do you think you are?'

'Where are your manners?'

'You can't treat people like this.'

He let out a growl and said, 'Oh yes, you sold a copy of Graham Greene's *The Quiet American*. I've left the money on the desk.'

'Thank you and I am sorry,' I said, but he wasn't listening. He was hurrying down the road, acting as if he was late for his own wedding.

When I walked inside the bookshop, there was a different atmosphere from the usual comfort. I didn't know how to continue. I felt like taking myself off to another place. I wanted to walk back outside, beyond the horizon and the perimeters of space and time. Everything, pressing against me like the walls in a nightmare. I wondered whether I should continue at all. All because of a robbery. The theft of a bag, of a photograph.

Silly really. But that's how I felt.

'Are you okay?'

I looked up blankly.

'You seemed to be in another world.'

It was Hannah.

'No, I was just thinking of visiting one,' I replied quietly.

I told her what had happened that morning, how the robbery had led to me questioning my faith in everything.

'I feel jolted. Jilted and very confused. It's as if my nightmare, which I covered for so long, has veered off in a new direction. Does that make sense?'

I was looking straight at her. She listened intently. Now and again, I wanted to say more but nothing would come out. Then I spoke words that didn't relate to what I was trying to say, and I'd apologise for my confusion.

There was no judgment on her face. She just listened to my story.

Finally I spoke of my drive up to Scotland, expecting to find Luke, wanting to take care of him, to keep him warm. I hadn't spoken of it in years. But it seemed right to talk to Hannah. It was that experience of how, when we open up to someone, it surprises us how honest we're being, the unforeseen familiarity.

She closed her eyes and took a deep breath. She opened them. I looked at her and she looked back at me. We were like, when one person leans enquiringly out of a window, someone at the same time leans out of the one right next to it.

'I've got to go,' she said, quite suddenly, and then asked, 'Have you had your lunch?'

'No. I'm not hungry.'

It was a white lie. I was famished but didn't want to be seen as a burden.

I pulled at the door. It had suddenly become very heavy and appeared to be stuck. It opened a sliver, then banged back. I pulled again.

I felt like a competitor in a tug of war.

'Here, let me do it,' said Hannah.

She turned the latch and it opened easily.

'Remember I'm here for you,' she said, smiling gently.

∴

I picked up the money for *The Quiet American*, which had been stacked on the table. The paperback had been paid for in pound coins. I opened the till and poured in the change. The till was an old one, the type where you have to push down hard on the numbered key to bring up the price and get the drawer to open. It gave the impression no sale was easy. I didn't care that my nostalgia was impractical. It had become an integral part of the shop.

The weeks after I signed the lease had been a blur, other than packing and unpacking, packing again, sleeping, waking, sleeping again. I remembered little. It was as if I'd been locked in solitary confinement, where I'd been making plans for my future and miraculously, when I was released, all my plans had been hatched.

The shop had been completely gutted and remodelled. I wanted it to represent everything, not just a place to buy books but also a refuge; a space you could walk into and find any world – or word – you desired.

I positioned a small sign above the door: *The Past is Present. Even Nothingness is part of Everything.*

Julia, after we reconnected at the party, had become a wonderful friend again. She checked on me with a daily telephone call and we'd go out to dinner, or see the occasional film. She helped out with the shop, advising me on setting up the business. She'd worked at Foyles for a year, after Edinburgh University, so she had the knowledge to order stock and teach me the basic rules.

I see the miracle in her now, being there at that time. I appreciated her support but can't remember if I said so. She interested me. She even intrigued me. I didn't want to be interested and certainly not intrigued, not yet, if ever. It was too early for that.

And where are you now, dear Julia? For you did suddenly disappear.

'We can't just be friends.'

You were probably right.

I stretched the elastic band I was fiddling with, a finger at each end. It snapped.

'*Ow!*'

I sat up as if I had no choice. I felt like an oversized puppet hoisted by ropes. What was I doing sitting here?

I had to go out and find the photograph.

∴

The streets were bustling. The sun had brought out the city.

Where do I begin my hunt? Perhaps where the crowds sit outside to eat and drink in the square? That's where the pickpockets work, isn't it? Or will they be operating where the crowd keeps moving?

Too much choice can be bewildering.

'Think of an example,' the teacher snaps and the mind goes blank. 'Choose a number,' you say, and the delinquent dithers. 'Think of anyone,' we get told, and we gallop through galleries.

My father warned me about pickpockets before I went travelling on my gap year. I'd decided to visit South America and my father had sat me down the day before I left to pass on his knowledge of 'foreign climes' as he called them.

Pickpockets were first on his agenda.

'Never carry too much cash. If you do, divide it up. Keep some inside your sock, not just inside your shoes because the whores always look there, so if you're mugged, you've enough money to pay for a taxi back to your hotel.'

Unfortunately I didn't listen and, by the end of my first night in Bolivia, I'd been robbed and beaten up until I was unconscious. I woke up in hospital. A nurse with eyes the colour of jade took care of me.

'Please, stay at my apartment for as long as it takes you to get well,' she offered.

I did. But that's another story.

As a finale to the father and son chat, which was probably the only one we ever shared, he spoke of whores and indulged my curiosity.

'Only when I travelled did I meet any of those sort,' he admitted, in the most disingenuous manner.

I was dying to interrupt him and ask a thousand questions but I knew, if I did, he would dry up.

In the end, he gave the following advice.

'Never go for the good-looking ones. They're likely to have been with a lot of men and will probably give you the clap.'

I was unable to keep quiet. I questioned whether there was any pleasure to be found in going with ugly women. I also made the simple observation that, if everyone followed his rule, the good-looking girls would have no clients and therefore would be the safest of all.

'Don't be clever,' my father replied.

∴

I headed towards the square. Faces and more faces. Then I caught the quickest look of a woman who seemed familiar to me. I turned away, then turned again to see the back of her head.

I dithered. *Is that one of them?*

Go on, follow her, I urged myself. *What have you got to lose?*

I started to walk, five paces behind. I found my view blocked by a small group huddled around a priest, who was wearing a black leather jacket and dog collar. He was reading from a Bible. His audience stood around him with their heads bowed, lips at times mouthing unheard words. One of them then took a few paces towards the road, to place a wreath of red and white flowers down by the curb.

'What happened here?' I asked, half-knowing the answer.

'A cyclist was mowed down at this exact spot yesterday. The bastard didn't even stop.'

He shuffled uneasily. His breathing became heavier, a mixture of hate and excitement, as if he were about to announce that the killer should be strung up, when we were distracted by someone tying a photograph to a lamppost. It showed a lovely young girl with a slender neck, her skin flawless and white as a shroud, her flowing black hair touching her shoulders. She stared into the lens with iridescent eyes and now, years later, she stared out from the spot where she'd been killed.

I hadn't thought of the victim being a girl.

I just presumed it was a young man with a thick mane of brown hair.

I immediately recognised the mother. She had the same eyes as her daughter and the same analgesic ires that I have, that Hannah has, that anyone who's lost someone close has. She would carry them for the rest of her life.

She looked at me and I instinctively flashed an 'I'm terribly sorry' look. I wanted to say, 'I understand,' but I stood back. It was none of my business.

So I moved on.

∴

The likelihood of finding the woman I'd glimpsed earlier was remote. Anyway, it probably wasn't her. How many times do we think we've caught sight of the person we've come to meet off a bus or train, only to find it's not them?

I decided to walk back to the church. Perhaps she'd gone there to ask for forgiveness or meet her friend.

Catch the two together. Now that would be something.

The sun was getting warmer. The small park nearby was even more full than before. An old man was trying to pull a deck chair from the pile. I saw the number on the side. It was, of course, number sixty-six. He opened his chair with surprising ease and, when he sagged into it, he looked up at me.

'One of the few things we cannot be accused of or blamed for is how old we are,' he said.

'That's an old quote,' I replied.

'It's true, though.'

He was dressed in a Hawaiian shirt and yellow shorts. His flesh was very white and hairless; a rather sickly sight, like the soft underbelly of a crocodile. He was sweating slightly.

'You look as if you're searching for something.'

'Yes,' I said. 'A thief!'

I moved on, sharpish, sensing he was a bore, perhaps so bored he'd lost the initiative to do anything to address his boredom.

∴

I'd lost myself in the crowd. For only a couple of seconds I didn't know where I was, but it felt like an eternity. The full glare of the sun was blazing down on my head.

Damn, I thought. *I should've worn a hat.*

I needed to sit down. I was beginning to sweat and lose heart, thinking I'd no chance of finding those thieves. I felt like a child who'd lost his mother.

I needed a drink.

'You wouldn't mind getting me a bottle of water?' I asked a woman.

She didn't hear me. She was too busy reading her book. She was concentrating so hard, it struck me she may have been feigning.

'You wouldn't mind getting me a bottle of water,' I asked, this time a little louder.

But again she paid no attention. This time not only because she was reading, but because she was busy shooing away what looked like horseflies from her breasts, which the insects had probably mistaken for a horse's rump.

She looked up and peered at me inquisitively.

'What are you looking at?' she snapped.

'I'm feeling a little faint. It really is hot. I need a glass of water or anything.'

And with that she suddenly slammed her book shut, got up and walked over to the makeshift bar set up by the entrance. I watched as she carefully tiptoed over dozens lying flat on their backs half-asleep, their faces turned towards the sun with mouths wide open.

Watch out for those horseflies, I thought.

∴

'Have this on me,' she said, passing over an ice-cool bottle of Pepsi Cola.

I gulped it down and it worked a miraculous cure.

'I needed that,' I said. 'Thank you.'

And instead of saying 'not a problem,' or 'on second thoughts you owe me one-fifty,' she let out a surprisingly deep laugh that sounded like a tap not quite turned off.

'What were, or rather what are, you reading?' I asked.

She held up Graham Greene's *The Quiet American*.

Another of life's coincidences.

'I got it from the library. I suffer an addiction to books.'

'Bibliolatry,' I replied.

'Exactly. I'm forever searching for that one book,' she said.

'Have you ever got near to finding it?'

'Finding what?'

'Why, that one book, of course.'

'Sometimes I have. Sometimes I was certain I had. But then I'd change my mind and think, I'm coming to the conclusion it doesn't exist. It's like true love. It's an endless quest.' And then she exclaimed, with a tremor in her voice, 'But the journey is better than arriving.'

I was about to agree when, in the corner of my eye, I glimpsed the woman I'd seen earlier. It was the thief! She was in the line for an ice cream and, would you believe it, she was showing my photograph to a friend. Her black hair looked different. It had been straightened and fell over her shoulders.

I calmed myself. My inner voice said, *Go and get her.*

I turned in her direction. She was there. She was still there.

'Hey you!' I shouted, and started to barge my way through the sun-seeking crowd.

'Hey, watch yourself,' someone yelped, as I stood on his stomach. 'Where's your respect?'

'Thief!' I shouted.

As I rushed up to her, I put my hand on her shoulder like an arresting policeman. 'Give me back my photograph!'

She brushed my hand off. I held out my other, still not sure whether we were on stage or in the foyer, as it were.

'You're a thief,' I said, with enough seriousness in my voice to suggest I didn't want the scene to continue as pure theatre.

I held her arm, this time with the grip of a vice.

'Let go of me!' she yelled.

Her friend – not the same one she'd been with earlier – started to slap me on my back, like in a Punch and Judy show.

'Get off her, old man!' the friend yelled at the top of her voice. She was so loud, the entire park stopped and turned in our direction.

The park attendant walked up and calmly asked what was going on.

'This woman is a thief. She stole that photograph from me.'

The attendant tried to unpeel my fingers from her arm.

'Let go, sir.'

I could feel my fingertips digging deeper into her flesh.

'All right,' I said, reluctantly letting go of her arm.

She leaned forward provocatively in a way that suggested she was either going to spit or give me a full kiss on the mouth.

'It was her,' I said.

'Maybe it was someone like her,' said the attendant.

'No, it is her.'

'Can you prove it?'

'I can. The photograph is of me and my son.'

'Let me see the photograph, please,' the attendant said, in a manner suggesting he'd asked for something like this before.

The woman resisted and held it to her chest.

'Madam, please, or I will have to call the police.'

'I want you to call the police,' she replied. 'I've just been assaulted, for God's sake.'

'Rubbish,' I interrupted.

'If you're so innocent, show us the photograph!' a voice in the crowd shouted. *'People like you should be locked up!'*

'Hand it over, you bitch!' another voice yelled.

The attendant turned to the crowd.

'Careful, sir,' he said. 'You could end up doing time, using language like that.'

The row seemed to unify the park. Anything for entertainment, a bit of communal fun.

'Don't all shout out at once, please,' the attendant said, half-heartedly.

No one was paying him any attention. The mob had already reached their verdict and this woman, this dark-haired woman with straight black hair to her shoulders, was guilty.

'I said would everyone please … *Shut up!*'

There was a moment's pause. It was as if the attendant had finally found his voice.

'Are you in the habit of stealing things?' he asked rhetorically, flummoxed. 'For example, other people's pictures? I ought to warn you, you won't get away with it. Your best option is to show me the photograph.'

His newfound confidence was suddenly gleaming.

She hesitated, looked at the photograph and then grudgingly handed it over.

He inspected it like a judge examining some piece of evidence just before passing it over to the jury.

'What is your photograph of?' he asked me.

'It's of my son … and of me.'

My voice broke, knowing the photograph was within reach.

He hesitated, as if he was about to let too big a cat out of its bag.

Get on with it. Have no fear. I shall forgive her.

He paused further.

There are those who enjoy the white-knuckle rides at the fun fair, and those who do not. This creature is, I lay a bet, a champion of the latter. *'Wheeeeee!'* some people squeal at the top of the steep slope, while our uniformed friend would have his eyes closed, teeth clenched, muttering, 'This is one of my definitions of hell.'

He held his breath and then stuttered, 'I'm a-f-fraid…' He held up the photograph. 'This can't be yours.'

He was right. It was of a baby, not older than a few weeks, sucking his or her dummy.

My head bowed.

'Shame on you. Shame! Shame on you!' said the pockmarked face.

The crowd started to stir. It began to hiss and boo, people's allegiance turning.

'Thank you,' the woman said, snatching back the photograph. She turned to me, 'You ought to be arrested. I've a good mind to ask the police to escort your old arse to the cells. You stupid, lonely old git!'

She was no longer the girl who had robbed me that morning.

'Shame on you for accusing an innocent mother,' said the woman who, only a few minutes before, had treated me to a bottle of Pepsi. She waved her book at me frenetically, like a dowager in a hot theatre.

'Shame … shame … shame …,' the crowd jeered.

The attendant then gave a strangely abrupt cough, and leaned towards me.

'I would get out of here if I were you, sir.'

'But I …'

'Sir, you should leave.'

I walked away as unflustered as possible.

Throughout my first years of grieving, I'd been assured that the brain had its own defence mechanisms and could blot out anything too powerful for it to handle. In the first weeks after

Luke was murdered, I'm sure it was true. My brain protected me or else I wouldn't have been able to go on. Even now, it still seems a miracle I did. But as I walked into the church for refuge rather than prayer, the pain was so acute, the disappointment so overwhelming, that I slumped into the nearest pew and wept.

I wept until it hurt.

∴

My flat was hellishly stuffy. It was as if, with a click of a finger, the air conditioning had been turned from cold to hot: winter, rendered as midsummer. The hour I spent in church had helped restore enough strength for me to make it back home but I longed for the solitudinous peace of distant waves, to get away, in truth to find an ocean. My faith had evaporated. I no longer had the desire to go on.

I dabbed my forehead with a paper towel. It was as if I'd too much sun. I had to pinch myself to realise, what had happened had really happened.

Screams, hisses, shrugging of shoulders, discussing me.

'Who was that crazy man?'

'Shame!'

As I'd walked away, the shameful chorus had followed me into the church. They couldn't realise, the photograph was my last physical link to my son. Who would understand? No one. Just me.

I looked out of my window. There had been a promise of rain to cool down the city. The clouds were in a stage of chaos but there was no rain, no lightning, nor any thunder. Perhaps a film would take me out of my reality. I searched among my DVDs for the right title. My other voice started a conversation.

'How about a movie tonight?'

'What's on?'

'Who knows?'

'Who cares?'

'What about this one?'

'*The Constant Complainer.* Sorry, I mean *The Constant Gardener.*'

'Definitely, yes!'

I took the disc out of its case and switched on the player. I loaded the disc into the tray and dimmed the lights down. The movie started with a hush. When I'd tried to it at my local cinema, the man next to me, who'd evidently seen it before, didn't seem to care that he was explaining, rather loudly, to his neighbour who'd not seen the film before and was hard of hearing, or stupid or both, each of the scenes before they happened. He wouldn't shut up, so I walked out.

I sat up watching, unwrapping a sweet, and slowly unpeeling the paper with intended quiet as if in a cinema. I sneezed as I pulled my Coca-Cola top. I noticed how well all the actors looked and how infrequently, if at all, they sneezed, picked their noses or went to the bathroom. I had to reassure myself that the gunshots and screams were coming from the screen and not my imagination.

Before the end of the film, I'd fallen asleep. I was woken up by the machine switching itself off. I stood up, adjusted my eyes to the light of the moon that seemed small.

Not, I thought, *as small as it should be.*

That was my last thought of the day. I robotically walked to my bedroom, undressed and crashed out. I didn't even give myself time to tell God I hadn't forgotten what I'd said: if the photograph wasn't returned, I'd spend my last days on this earth as an unbeliever.

∴

I woke early the following morning. It had been a difficult sleep. I thought about pulling the blankets over my head and then regretted and resented. I cursed out loud, not only because another day had arrived but because I'd lost – and probably would never regain – my balance.

A simple robbery and I felt helpless.

I thought of turning over and trying to doze away into a wonderful world that was part-thought, semi-meditation, quasi-dream. Maybe that would give me peace. But no, there was a chill in the air like the desert at night but I knew the heat from the previous day would return later.

Ah, the utter quietness of it all.

I looked at the pile of novels perched on my bedside table. They lay beside my Bible, a well-thumbed pocket edition in black leather. I let out a sceptical sigh and sat up, piling the pillows behind my back. I reached for the remote and turned the TV on.

A presenter was chatting with two experts, a man and a woman, about the demise of family values. The man had what looked like a fake six-day beard growth darkened by the rub of a burned cork. The woman was dressed in an authoritative blue suit. They were spouting about respect and loyalty being the backbone of any good relationship. The fly crawled over the presenter's face and then, as if bored, it flew away.

Just as it did, I recognised the woman. It was Lady Sturgess, who lived on the neighbouring street and regularly popped into my bookshop for a natter. Lady Sturgess, who soon after her wedding confided to her friends that she'd made 'a terrible mistake' and was, from the beginning, reluctant to conceive children 'in case they end up too much like him, with weak chins.' For reasons never ascertained, though, she did in the end produce a pack of brats. She talked about them constantly, in their presence but as if they weren't there. She was forever tidying their hair in public while they cringed with embarrassment.

I was about to join the fly and get the hell out of my flat, when the phone rang.

'Hello,' I said turning down the volume on the television.

'I hope I'm not calling you too early?'

It was Hannah.

'Not at all, I've been up for … hours.'

'I wanted to invite you to breakfast. My treat.'

'Why?' I replied, rather too quickly.

'Because you looked as if you needed feeding yesterday. I was a bit worried about you.'

'It was a bad day,' I said. 'I lost faith in the world. I felt as if I'd reached rock bottom." I paused. 'Another rock bottom.'

I was surprised by my frankness.

'Don't worry. I'm sure it will get better. Sooner or later, things always do.'

'Let's hope so,' I said.

'Will I see you for breakfast, then?'

'You will,' I replied. 'And, thank you.'

'Good. We'll be open in half an hour. It looks like it's going be another scorcher.'

∴

There's a part of each of us in the past, another in the future. We have one foot in yesterday, one in tomorrow. We drag ourselves to the here and now.

I brushed my teeth as if they were linoleum, my face slowly as if it were marble. I looked at my eyes in the mirror. *Dear Lord! Why is it the start of the day, still, that I find so difficult? Oh God, what am I doing here on this earth? Doing here – and not doing here. Where is God, anyway? Or anyone who sets themselves up as comforter, explainer, definer, curer, guru, guide, saviour?*

Damn it! Forget them. Who needs that lot? We can all pray in our own way, call on that greatness out there, plug into the transcendental power of the universe, syphon towards the great singularity.

More simply put, we can each talk with our own guts.

Could I not go on praying, even when I felt nearly incapable of praying? I'd heard it said, to try to pray really is to pray. When someone says, 'If I prayed, I'd pray for you', he is, in fact, praying.

'We thy creatures, but miserable sinners, do in this our great distress cry unto thee for help. Save Lord, or else we perish …'

I tried to move but couldn't. I'd found solace after Luke had died but now I felt it was just a prop to keep me standing.

How can a small act of robbery fracture my belief? Perhaps it was never there and I fooled myself because I needed to.

That was an excruciating thought.

∴

As I walked to the elevator, I nearly collided not with the Colonel but my next-door neighbour. I'd nicknamed him the Early Riser because he started his day at the eccentric hour of two o'clock in the morning. Yes, two! I'd once seen him waiting for the lift at that time.

'Good evening,' I said.

'You mean good morning,' he replied. 'I understand you were robbed yesterday.'

'Yes,' I replied.

'I'm sorry to hear that. I truly am. Do you know, when the morning is at its most still, when we can say we're past that exact moment when night turns into morning, it's your bookshop that shines the most among all the other buildings – like a bright star.'

And I said without thinking, 'That's my son watching over it …'

He didn't say anything but walked towards his front door. Just as he took out his key, he turned to me.

'It's a fine day out there. You should try to enjoy it.'

There were no free tables outside Hannah's restaurant. Two men were occupying a table that seated six. I asked them whether they minded if I joined them.

'Not at all,' one smiled.

I stammered a silence and sat uneasily into my chair. At first I refused to look at them then pretended not to. They were an odd couple, Ugh and Yuk. The one closest to me, Mr Ugh, had the too-cherubic smile of someone who was about to commit, or had just committed, indeed was in the process of committing some antisocial, perhaps criminal, act.

His friend, Mr Yuk, had the hairiest hands I'd ever seen: so hirsute, had anyone disputed the claim that humankind evolved from apes, I'd have pointed to Mr Yuk as indisputable proof of the fact.

'We fly to Italy tomorrow and look at the bloody forecast,' said Ugh, holding up his *Daily Mail*. 'It's like a fridge over there, for God's sake!'

He threw over the newspaper.

'It says Florence is 17 degrees Celsius. That's not too bad,' said Yuk.

'Not too bad, you say?' Ugh snatched his paper back. 'Well, the weather will need to be much warmer before I use the swimming pool, thank you. Things will need to hot up before I'll even begin to enjoy myself.'

'Assuming it does.'

'Assuming you do.'

'What you mean by that?'

Ugh coughed loudly to draw the attention of the waitress. He pointed at his cup, signalling for more coffee.

I opened my book and tried to read.

'You get more tanned from filtered sunlight,' said Ugh, so loudly that the whole street could hear.

'It's more agreeable not to lie in the full glare.'

'Of the sun, or of life?'

'Oh, leave us in peace, philosopher.'

I was about to depart without even ordering when I saw Hannah's smiling face heading in my direction.

'Everything all right?'

I both nodded and shook my head, like a nervous schoolboy. She immediately understood and clicked her fingers. Very quickly, an extra table was set up. The edges verged to the outside of my store.

'Could you bring me a coffee, please?' I asked.

A dog walker had stopped at the table of Ugh and Yuk and they'd started a conversation. Although I'd moved far enough away for most people not to hear what they were saying, snatches of their conversation hovered up into the blue sky and blasted back in my direction.

'And how have you two spent the day?' the dog walker asked. 'Still in love?'

'Wouldn't you like to know?'

'Mind your own business!'

'Voyeur!'

'Voyeuse!'

I chuckled to myself, sweet trivia distracting me from the day ahead. Hannah served me a bowl of muesli with my coffee. She started to talk. I was listening but I heard nothing.

'So sorry,' I said. 'What did you say?'

It was like reading a passage of a book, but then realising I hadn't taken in a single word.

'Not important,' she replied.

'This is very kind of you.'

Hannah put a finger to lips. My lips! She looked into my eyes, my tired eyes, and smiled. 'Ssshhh, no more of that,' she said. 'Eat up. It'll do you good.'

∴

I vowed to do no more thinking for a while. To think is to do. To think is to be. You are what you think, although you are, perhaps, not what you think you are.

Sweat trickled down my forehead and through my lashes. Fleas were out in force. I slapped my hand against my arms and legs, sometimes so hard that blood burst from one of the beasts spurting blood over my skin.

Stop it, Mr Hammond. We are all God's creatures.

I was leaving some money to cover my breakfast when Hannah came out.

'Nothing to pay,' she said. 'I told you, this is on me.'

She disappeared inside and returned with a glass of cold water.

'You look hot. Drink this.'

She was right. I slugged it down and in that instant drowned my vow. Damn it! I vowed not to think and ended up thinking even more.

'Don't overdo it today. The heat is intense,' Hannah said.

I smiled. For a moment I saw her striding towards a swimming pool, pulling off her towelling robe. There she stood, ready to take the plunge: full-breasted, long-legged.

Dive, dive, dive ...

I imagined the softness of her breasts against my chest, in my hands; her wet hair falling all over her face, dripping globules of water into my mouth ...

So. I was alive, after all.

'Tom!'

Hannah's voice interrupted my thoughts.

I briefly closed my eyes to regain some composure and breath. Without another word, I walked away, as if holding onto a rope that was frayed from a thousand clutchings by people similar to me.

I wasn't going to open the shop today. I was going in search of the photograph again.

In a very short space of time, I'd tried to think of nothing, wallowed in a fantasy and now felt flat – as low as when I'd woken up a few hours before. Luke's face from his last night, from that photograph, loomed before my eyes, submerging my thinking; Luke, the age I'd last seen him at the airport, his handsome face.

'Whoever we are, we're all nudging towards death, Daddy. Don't forget.' I heard the faint voice whisper in my ear. 'We're all getting older.'

I reached the top of the street and already felt uneasy, like I was driving a car by the side of a lake and taking sharp turns in a thick mist. I regretted not picking up a bottle of water. I felt I was starting to hallucinate. Crowds were already enjoying yet another fine warm day with muted conversations and conspiracies; banging doors that sounded like gunshots; the whirr of air conditioning and gases; rushing sounds travelling down pipes, water washing bodies already poisoned, shot, drowned in baths, under showers …

'Easy does it,' I said, trying to console myself with a dry tongue.

Find those women; find the photograph.

It was time to find another drink of water, quickly. No sooner had I left one restaurant, I was in search of another. I meandered from street to street. The cafés were overflowing with customers, all telling their stories loudly and non-stop. It was as if they knew others were waiting like jackals for their moment to pounce, hardly listening to what was being said, already sure of what they'd say once the storyteller offered them a chink of a chance. Then, as I glimpsed a free table in a sheltered corner, a gust of wind moaned as if in mourning and I felt myself losing balance. It was as if I'd been standing on a train and got thrown off my feet by a sudden lurch.

I fell down to the ground, the sun ceasing to breathe without revealing its secrets.

The next thing I remember, I was lying in a bed, in hospital.

Hannah was staring down at me.

∴

'Where am I?' I asked her.

'St George's.'

'How did I get here?'

'By ambulance. When you collapsed, someone called 999. A local recognised you and went to your shop to tell somebody what had happened. As everything was shut, she came next door and told me.'

I pulled the blanket up to my neck. Hannah put the back of her hand to my forehead. Her touch surprised me, her obvious care moved me, unbearably. I hadn't felt a touch like that for a long time.

I closed my eyes and slowly opened them again, gradually focusing on the light above my bed. I could smell Hannah. Her scent was the sweet smell of honeysuckle.

I am stumbling through a field, a Scottish meadow.

'Why run?' a voice echoes.

Although there is no breeze, the leaves on the trees are rustling like a ship's rigging. I feel no fear. A light flashes in the distance.

Is that my son? Is it Luke?

I notice a figure at intervals, disappearing and reappearing behind the trees and in the long grass. It isn't someone like him. There is no one like him. No one walks like that, no one walked like that, no one will ever walk like that. Just as I'm getting closer and closer, he is gobbled up by the horizon.

I stand still and look up at the sun. I try to speak but I can't.

I can't even say, 'I miss you. I miss you very day, every second, every minute …'

∴

The noise of a rattling trolley woke me up. I felt I'd been asleep for an hour. I was told later I'd been in hospital for six days. What a dream. I watched with one eye open as a surly domestic steered a trolley as if she were riding a dodgem car at the funfair. She huffed and puffed as patient after patient seemed to get in her way. When I opened my other eye, Hannah was looking down at me. It seemed this wasn't the first time I'd been awake in the six days, because she acted as if we'd had a conversation only hours earlier.

The domestic flumped down a plate of food. It was sea grey, tough or soggy, undercooked or overcooked.

'God, no.' I pushed the plate away as if I were a child.

'You really should eat, Tom,' Hannah said.

Life suddenly froze and all I could hear was the sound of the other patients murmuring half-complaints. Then I heard a voice that jerked me out of my daze.

'How are you doing?' asked a doctor with tousled golden hair that made him look like he belonged on a Californian beach.

I thought, *Are you really a doctor?*

He fixed a smile on me and then spoke in riddles. I tried to follow what he was saying to me but throughout his 'you were dehydrated, had an infection, need to drink a lot of liquid, very weak, have to look after yourself ' speech, my head swayed. It was if I were on a ship in the middle of a storm, hanging onto the railings with all my strength to stop myself falling into the sea. The doctor's speech continued but now his mouth moved like a dummy held by a vain ventriloquist, sounding out one wordless word at a time.

'He's right. You need rest,' Hannah said.

'What I need is to get out of here. I have to find my photograph. I have to find the photograph,' I said, repeating the last line so often it became a mantra.

Hannah looked at the doctor, I looked at Hannah.

'It hasn't been found, has it?'

She shook her head and put her hand on my shoulder offering sympathy.

'I'm afraid not,' she answered.

'Just a few more days and I'm sure you'll be fine to go home,' the doctor said.

With that he turned on his suede brogues and moved on, to the next bed.

'Are you really a doctor?' I overheard my neighbour ask.

Ha!

'I can't stay here,' I said impatiently. I stood up with remarkable ease, because I knew in that moment what I had to do.

My clothes were neatly laid out on the chair next to the bed. I started to get dressed.

∴

Hannah shared the short taxi ride home. I did have to sign a release form stating it was my decision, blah blah blah, and I was responsible for my life. They did insist I ate something before I left, which I agreed to. I chose some breakfast cereal and a piece of toast, munching away grudgingly as they sorted out the details.

I thanked Hannah for being my friend and I was about to say, 'You're the most adorable gift' – but I didn't, because she was years younger than me and, boringly, I didn't think it was appropriate to say.

Instead I simply said, 'Thank you'.

'Don't you think people come into your life when you most need them?' she replied.

Yes. They do. For a moment she changed, from a confident woman into a young girl unsure of herself, grabbing her handbag with both hands.

As the taxi drove off, I caught her face looking out to make sure I was alright. I did feel a little tired, as well as angry that there was no still no sign of the photograph. I knew from my past that anger led me into the darkness. How does that dreary phrase go?

Anger is only one letter short of Danger.

I wanted to head out and start my search all over again but, by the time I'd even thought of opening the front door, I felt tired and in need of more rest.

My bed was still unmade. I undressed and crawled into it, then immediately crawled out again and knelt down on shaking knees. I prayed out loud and sighed as I looked at my worn Bible. I never defined my belief, thinking to do so would be an affront to the indefinable. I felt by joining the ranks of one particular faith we were propagating divisions – and the more fanatical, the deeper the divisions we caused by rendering something as exclusive.

∴

Over the following days, I ate little. I could hear myself start to take slow and shallow breaths. I was breathing unevenly, my shoulders slumped, muscles tightened.

My regular calls to the police were answered in an apologetic tone, at first.

'I'm very sorry. No news, I'm afraid ...'

They became more abrupt, though.

'We are still looking.'

I stopped making calls when I overheard the policeman on duty, when he failed to put the phone down properly, talking to his colleague.

'It was the crackpot again,' he said. 'Calling about the photo of his dead son.'

My sister must have sensed something was wrong, because she rang and kept on ringing until I answered.

'I'm fine, don't worry.'

But she didn't believe me. She always had an incredulous look on her face whenever I said things were alright. To quote the clairvoyant's card, *Each day in the past fades a little. Time heals, but does not cure.*

My sister still lived in Cornwall, in the same house. Her family had remained healthy and prosperous.

'At least, one of us isn't cursed,' I once said.

She got angry, surprised, concerned. 'Don't talk rubbish,' she said, not believing it. But what else could she say? 'Yes, you're right. To lose your child must mean you're cursed. That your life has gone silent.'

'I can hear something in your voice. What happened?' my sister asked.

'I was robbed.'

'What was stolen?'

'A photograph. The one taken on Luke's last night.'

'Oh, Tom,' she said, immediately understanding how painful it must have been.

'I went to church and told God believing had been a waste of time, that I didn't deserve any more pain.'

'Don't lose hope in your heart, Tom,' my sister said, sounding more like a priest than a housewife overlooking Daymer Bay. 'Everything will turn out alright.'

'I don't think so.'

'Be kind to yourself, Tom. Don't presume anything.'

'I have to go. I've a friend coming over.'

'A friend?'

'Goodbye …'

'Did you say friend?'

'Bye …'

'I'll call in a couple of days …'

Click.

I picked up the book of quotes sitting right in front of me and opened it, playing that game where the first one you read is your lesson for the day. It was Kahlil Gibran's *'When you are sorrowful, look again in your heart, and you shall see that in truth you are weeping for that which has been your delight.'* – and perhaps that said it all.

∴

Charles was staring out of the shop window, fiddling with a piece of paper in his left hand. It seemed to have been folded many times. Since his return from holiday, he would make new gestures with his hands, suggesting some change had taken place inside him.

'Did you know,' I began, 'if you were capable of folding a piece of paper just forty-two times, it would reach to the moon?'

I was sitting with my elbows on the armrests of my chair, looking at a book with philosophical questions printed in a large, Baskerville font.

Are we born with a conscience? Should morality be taught or caught, or both, or neither? I was just looking at the words, my mind fading into the shadowlands of the printed page. It had been six weeks since the robbery and still nothing had been recovered. My faith had gradually begun to crumble, the threat of taking my last breath as a disbeliever coming true. There were moments I'd tried to come to terms with the past, so that I'd be able to face each new day – but it was no good, I seemed not to have any strength left and it was beginning to show physically. I'd lost weight and was looking gaunt.

Each day Charles wanted to speak with me but seemed unable to. He reminded me of someone who, for once in his life, had the right answer in class but couldn't bring himself to raise his hand or call out.

I was beginning to live as if I knew when my last day in life was going to be. It was as if I was cheating, reading the last line of a book first. I knew how it was going to end.

Charles was seated opposite me and was sorting the new publications. It was as if we were in a library – *Sshh, be quiet!* – while he piled the books with his right hand and carried on folding the paper with his left.

He must be one of those people who do things with both, I thought.

As he continued to look through the titles, he crumpled the folded piece of paper into a ball and flicked it, as if he was playing table soccer. I caught it before it fell symbolically on the table. I looked at the paper and started to unravel it but it was empty. Not a word written on it. I thought of tearing it up, into many little pieces. I didn't, though. Instead, I refolded it as it had been folded before.

Another quote came to mind.

Whatever you do in life you should do it right, even if it is sometimes wrong.

I looked up. Hannah had appeared. Charles greeted her breathless, colourless, everythingless. He was clearly excited by her presence, or maybe by the fact that it meant the silence could be broken.

'How is everything?' Hannah asked.

'The same,' Charles replied, mumbling under his breath like a camel might, glancing at me with one eye as if I were a hopeless case.

It seemed to me that he'd grasped the nettle, that his job wasn't to sell books but to care for this lonely, sick and sad man.

'You don't look well,' Hannah said to me.

'I haven't been well for years,' I said, listening to my words slowly. The substance of what I was saying registered with me not immediately, but seconds later.

I got up and walked out of the shop without another word. Hannah wanted to grab me by the arm but Charles held her back. He was right to do so. I needed to get out. I needed to be alone again.

∴

I walked along the Embankment to the sound of traffic and a murmur of half-accusations. I was heading to nowhere in particular but, if you walk along the river long enough, the fumes will eventually force you to cross one of the bridges.

The day had turned humid, still without a breath of wind. Albert Bridge was deserted. It had been closed to traffic for so long, the cars had found a different route. As I stood looking out towards the Chelsea harbour, I thought, *What a delicious escape this is. I only wish I were strong enough to enjoy it.*

The silence was broken by the sound of grumbling old men, except that wasn't it at all – it was a dredger, chugging around, picking up dregs from the Thames riverbed. The south bank of the river was a scrapyard of assorted oddities from the inevitable bicycles and lamps to a school desk, clothes, single shoes and suitcases.

'Look at the thick mud.'

The voice belonged to a child about five years old.

Standing beside me were a father and son, close enough that if I reached out I'd be able to touch the father's shoulder.

Their proximity didn't disturb me. It was welcome.

The father lifted the boy onto his shoulders to get a better view of the dredger's work. I looked at the boys' eyes, captivated as they were by the scene.

'Somewhere down there,' began the father, 'hidden deep in the mud is a Spanish galleon, full of gold coins.'

The boy paused for a moment. 'Do you mean treasure?'

'Yes.'

'In the mud?'

'Yes. The mud is too thick for divers, so they need this big machine.'

The boy's eyes widened. 'Can we help?'

'I think it's best to leave it to the experts, don't you?'

The boy was too excited to talk anymore. He just nodded and kept on gazing. Unbelievable.

After five minutes, the father said, 'We'd better be going. We should get to the park and eat our sandwiches.'

The boy nodded but then shook his head, reluctant to miss anything.

This will not be easy, I thought.

'Come on, let's go.'

The boy started to cry. 'I don't want to.'

The father put his son down against one of the disused tollbooths that had a wide shelf, so there was no danger.

'Aren't you hungry?'

'Yes,' the boy reluctantly answered, 'but, why don't we eat here and watch the big machine?'

We both looked at the boy's pleading face. As a father I recognised it. There could only be one answer. With that face, little boys usually get their own way.

'Let's see what we have,' said the father, kneeling down and opening his bag. It looked like an old-fashioned school satchel. He pulled out a roast- beef sandwich. 'Mmm, this looks delicious.'

The boy bit into the crusty bread, chewing and chewing again, not taking his eyes off the dredger. The father passed him a carton of orange juice and, without taking a breath, the boy sucked through the straw until it was finished. He let out a deep breath then, of satisfaction, and squealed with delight – a high-pitched sound, like a newly hatched bird.

The dredger had found something.

The men operating the machinery became animated. There was a great deal of shouting about this potential find. The workmen on the riverbank threw away their cigarettes and looked towards the river in anticipation.

Was it treasure? Was it a body? No. It was the carcass of a dodgem, probably a remnant from the old Battersea funfair. I'm not sure why but the build-up and the eventual absurdity of the find made the three of us start to laugh.

The boy's laughter rushed through my body.

I recognised that laugh. It was Luke's laugh.

The father looked at his watch. 'We'd better be going,' he said, reaching to carry his son down.

The son started to cry and stomped his foot on the ground. 'No!'

'Come on. We'll come back tomorrow. I'm sure they won't have found the treasure.'

'But what if they do?'

'They won't. It's a big river, one of the biggest in the world. They'll be looking for days.'

'How big?' the son asked.

'What?'

'How big is the river?'

'Enormous.'

'As big as the one we saw in the country?'

'First, that wasn't a river, it was a lake. But, yes. Easily.'

The boy stretched out his arms. 'This big?'

The father stretched out his arms wide too. 'This big!' he said.

'Promise we will come back?'

'I promise.'

The father knelt down and kissed his son on the forehead, then took hold of his small hand. They started to zigzag down towards Battersea Park, until the boy suddenly stopped and turned.

We locked eyes. His eyes were so green, so familiar.

I couldn't speak. His look dumbfounded me.

There was no wind, not even a hint of a breeze. Yet the leaves from the park, at least half a mile away, seemed to be rustling so vigorously, as if an invisible spirit was shaking them.

The boy turned again and continued his zigzag. His father kept a hold on his hand.

I gazed out at the river. I could hear my breathing and sensed peace in it. I was comfortable but sad. I looked to the bank and studied the junkyard that was forming, then followed a seagull as it hovered over the objects in hope of finding some scraps.

A workman was building a fire that seemed incongruous on one of the hottest days of the year, but this was England and the winter cold might only have been just a few days away. The fire could be a hobo's salvation.

Dust was everywhere but still no wind. Next to the fire was a bag.

My eyes gradually focused on the small bag.

A small bag that looked very similar to mine.

It couldn't be.

I stood up. I felt numb. I walked from the bridge, down the steps onto the dried bank, trying to keep calm but, in my hurry, I tripped and nearly fell.

I instinctively said sorry but nobody was looking or listening.

Two workmen, who only minutes before were yelling with excitement at a possible find, now looked bored and shrugged their shoulders, as if to say 'help yourself'.

I moved towards the bag, my bag. I picked it up like a man who's not sure if a snake is dead or not. The Union Jack was still visible. I peeled off the dirt and threw it into the river, the same gesture a priest would deploy when throwing pieces of earth onto a coffin in the grave. I opened it. The book was still inside. I pulled it out. It was just a sodden pile of paper. I dug deeper and felt a small pool of water.

I said a prayer. I asked for the photograph to be inside the bag.

'Please God, let me find it.'

And it was there. It was there, in one piece. I looked at it.

The picture had completely washed out. It had just a vague trace of two figures, no clue to anything else.

My head lowered but then I looked up, to the sky. Whether it was by chance or meant to be, I saw a bird of prey hovering. It suddenly came spiralling down towards me. I held the photograph tightly in my hand but it had no use for that; instead, in one action, it plucked a mouse from the ground that had been scurrying away from the river.

In one dramatic action, as if there'd been a sudden crash of cymbals followed by silence, I awoke from my nightmare. It had been so unexpected, it affected not so much my eyes as my ears.

∴

When I returned to the bookshop, loud music was blasting out from one of the houses directly opposite. It was the sort that makes snobs semi-jokingly question whether the orchestra is still tuning up or asking if the audience has gone berserk. Charles was waiting outside, looking up at where the noise was coming from. His eyes flickered. He ran next door to tell Hannah I was back.

There was no need. She'd been looking out for me.

'I found it,' I told her.

I passed the remnant of the photograph into her hands.

'Oh, Tom.'

'I'm okay,' I said, and meant it.

I don't need it anymore, I realised.

'I saw a boy on the bridge,' I said. 'He looked like Luke did, when he was that age. Do you know, he stared at me. It was as if I was seeing Luke again and I knew, in that moment, he never really went away. He's never really gone at all. He's here, deep in my heart. And no murderer, nothing, will ever be able to take that away.'

Hannah took me in her arms. She held me tight as the golden evening sun poured treacle over everything. It was more like a dawn than a sunset. I looked up at the sky and watched as a jet exuded a long line of vapour, like the train of a wedding dress.

I thought of my son and, although the image was no longer visible, I touched the photograph as reassurance.

He was close to me again.

∴

Epilogue

We were welcomed by an elderly gentleman. He handed us a service book and hymnal.

He was a parent of one of those murdered. I could tell. We shared the same eyes, the sense of something we could never put behind us.

One woman was having her patience tested by an onlooker, who insisted on giving her a helping hand. Another didn't look up, head lowered to avoid the stares of strangers. A small group hesitated outside the church waiting for the service to begin, perhaps contemplating their own mortality.

It felt cold in the chapel. I was starting to freeze. I was still unsure as to why I'd decided to return to Scotland after twenty-five years. I'd done enough grieving. I didn't need to share anymore, not with anyone – but the anniversary of that night made it important I was here. I'd always studiously avoided gatherings such as these. On each occasion, I was bereft. I grieved. My escape was someone sitting next to me, who had travelled as my support that morning.

Hannah rubbed my arm, sensing my chill. She'd first become my close friend and, to my surprise in the last month, we'd decided to get married.

I didn't know what she saw in me but I was blessed. Again. I'd found someone who helped me to continue to continue, to keep on keeping on, to finish the finishing to the beautiful or bitter end.

Father, Hear the Prayer We Offer and The Day Thou Gavest, Lord, is Ended were among the hymns we sang. They washed over me. Only a few words from a young woman, who lost her brother before she was born, resonated. She recited a poem she'd written the night before.

> *Perhaps I should try to explain*
> *How suddenly death can come*
> *Unless it is truly a real voyage*
> *Because a new one has begun.*

As we started to sing another hymn, my eyes were diverted by a sight that startled me out of any ingenuous belief that the rest of the service was going to be just more of the same. A beautiful woman was sitting a few pews ahead of us. She had devastating eyes of teak, a mane of lustrous brown hair. She wasn't singing the hymns; instead, she spent most of her time gazing up at the ceiling, as if she were avoiding the true pain of what was happening.

She sat alone. I instinctively knew she had nothing to do with her neighbour. There was something so familiar about her. I couldn't pinpoint what.

We all come from the same thing, the one all-acceptable definition of God.

A cacophonous organ chord signalled the end of the service. The congregation trooped outside onto the gravel. While we'd been in church, the afternoon sky had darkened and soon it would be as dark as when the plane, Pan Am 103, fell to the earth.

The parish church stood not far from where I'd arrived years before in search of my son. How different the place seemed now and yet, the same cold shudder ran through my body.

'Let's get out of here,' I was about say to Hannah, when I felt a small nudge on the back of my shoulder. I turned.

Facing me was the beautiful woman I'd noticed during the service.

'Mr Hammond?'

'Yes.'

'I'm Kate.'

And I said, instinctively, 'I know.'

Beautiful Kate, my son's love, the beautiful girl he was flying off to see. The girl who shared the same name as my late wife.

Luke's first and last love.

I hugged her so tightly.

'How have you been?' was my first question, I think.

Ah, the awkwardness of it all.

As I looked at her, I thought about the countless hours I'd imagined this very moment. Why didn't I go in search of her in all these years, dare to ask the questions I'd wanted to ask ever since I received her letter?

How are you, Kate? Are you healthy? Are you happy? Have you found another true love?

Go on, call her. Call her today.

What about the day the jets flew into the twin towers? Was she safe? Was she in the city? Did she see it and mourn her lost love, my son, killed years before in the same murderous, wicked fashion? Well, did you? Do you think of Luke like I do – every day?

So, why didn't I?

Why? Because I had to leave things alone. I didn't dare disturb anything. I bartered my curiosity for a peaceful mind. Like turning the pages of an old book with thin pages. I knew if I turned one, the paper would break apart and I'd never be able to piece the book back together again.

My fears were unjustified. She spoke freely about Luke. She talked about his smile, his humour, his cheekiness and then, without asking, she said something else.

'I got through those first years by moving forward at the same pace as Time. Therefore, paradoxically, I hardly noticed it.'

I thought, *What an extraordinary thing to say.*

I felt a chill. 'Come, we'd better get moving or we're all going to catch cold.'

'I'm all right. I have this to keep me warm,' said Kate.

She touched the navy blue polo neck sweater she was wearing. The very same sweater I'd bought for Luke and had taken to Scotland to keep him warm.

The sweater I sent to her shortly after he died.

My eyes welled up and I started to cry.

We decided to walk away from the church, to be nearer the mark where Luke's body was found. I never knew nor wanted to know the exact spot he fell but I understood it was near the town and close to a tree that was still standing. We walked by the plaques in Dryfesdale Cemetery, pausing to mark our respect to those fellow passengers who had all perished on December 21st.

At the end of the path, we opened a wooden gate and walked into a field. A beech tree stood proudly opposite to where we were standing. We paused and together looked up into the sky. It was a barrage of black at first, until one bright spark burst through, then another. And, gradually, there appeared a wellspring of stars, followed by galaxies galore and heavens innumerable.

The further you get from town, you know, the more stars you can see. Get out of the spotlight, away from the centre stage. Come out here to the dark wilderness, where there will always be more and more wonders to behold and glories to hear, smell, and feel.

This is the world we've been given. Through our shared tragedy, we were able in that moment to recognise it, in all its beauty.